MW01043550

Eight Jaguar
— or —
The Post-Modern Prometheus

By John Gamboa

PublishAmerica

Baltimore

© 2003 by John Gamboa.

First printing

ISBN: 1-4137-0552-9
PUBLISHED BY PUBLISHAMERICA, LLLP
www.publishamerica.com
Baltimore

Printed in the United States of America

Dedicated to Anne
who turned me into a human being

Introduction

Just the other day, my pretty wife told me that I was "becoming an ass."

When she said this, I had been watching TV, and I was really enjoying a documentary about World War Two. I used to not watch television very often, but lately I have been enjoying it, and making up for lost time. So I looked over at Minerva. She was brushing her pretty hair, and I was mesmerized by the sight. She normally has only the sweetest of words for me. I was trying to decide how to respond to her in a way that would address her statement, without initiating an argument. While I was busy thinking, she went on to pronounce that I had to "Do something about it."

I realized that I had to act quickly. I abandoned her insult and asked, "Do what, my darling?" This was risky, because I am learning that in a relationship, sometimes one is supposed to know exactly what to do or say, without asking. Apparently, asking reveals want of observational skills and thus narcissism. But I held my breath and waited.

She looked at me for a moment. "I want you to write out your story, Victor."

I skipped the part about what made her think that I could write anything more eloquent than the extremely ineloquent technical reports that I used to write. I also skipped the part about how writing my story would only provide potentially incriminating evidence. I did, however, mention that I have always doubted that 'journalizing' could be a substitute for therapy.

"I never said I want you to keep a journal," she said, defensively.

I asked her if she meant that I should write out what we had been through, like it was a book of fiction. She brushed her hair luxuriously. "Yes, but I want you to write the real story, instead of all the bullshit that the tabloids have printed. You know, Victor, the *story.*"

She suggested that stories like mine had been successful books, and that I might just get lucky, because according to her, the really badly written books seem to make the best movies. She brushed her hair some more and told me that the most important thing is that writing would keep me busy. I admitted that I was very bored, but I did not tell her that I was happy just watching lots of television. She finished brushing her hair silently, and then she pointed out that my story was all that I had left.

"Besides, it's all you have left," she said.

I repeat this last statement verbatim, because I had never considered my situation in this light. Of course, she was right. I asked my beloved if I should use a pen or a pencil. She pointed to the laptop computer that I have been carrying around with me. She calls it my "football," and jokes that I would handcuff myself to it if I had handcuffs. I would. The laptop is an older model, and it looks like it has been on a long camping trip, which, of course, it has. The hard drive in its guts contained some extremely valuable files. In fact, its memory was completely full. I patiently reminded Mini that it was not available for use as a word processor, and that it contained certain data files that…

"Dump the files."

She leaned her head to the side and pulled the brush down through her hair once more.

"But you know what's on here! These files are all we've got!" I was whining, and I stopped quickly, because she does not like it when I whine, and I try very hard to please her in every possible way. She looked at me with her "mind control" stare, and it was then that I realized that I was, perhaps, "acting like an ass" at that very moment. "No, Victor, your story is all you've got. No one can take that from you."

I hung my head in mock shame. I asked her if erasing my critical files and writing a book would help me to not "be an ass" anymore. She said it would. And since I love my insistent wife dearly, and since

I generally do everything she says, I deleted twenty-seven priceless files relating to a surgical procedure that people have literally killed for. Now this story is the only part of the whole fiasco that I have as evidence that any of it ever happened at all. And I have to admit; there is a part of me that is just itching to tell the story. And she's right. Those files needed to be trashed. I want nothing more to do with them.

Chapter 1: My Childhood

If indeed I am becoming unpleasant, it is only because I am being forced into an unnatural condition of inactivity. Yes, I have been compelled by circumstances to live the tortured existence of the idle workaholic. Perhaps this writing project will amend my shattered sense of purpose. Perhaps.

I spend so much of my time wondering where I went wrong. I'll start way back at the beginning. When I get to that point where I strayed from the virtuous and ethical path that I always assumed I was on, it will seem obvious. Together, we will discover my lapse of judgment.

I always thought that I had a normal childhood, but now I can see clearly that it must not have been entirely normal. It was only a normal childhood for a kid who preferred to read alone indoors over playing outside with other kids, who was not a participator, but an observer, who had taken up a very early and completely overwhelming fascination with the surgeons' craft. Sure, I know what you are thinking… lots of kids dig gory things. Monsters, war movies, blood and guts. But I was different. I liked *surgery*. Every year, I was a surgeon for Halloween. The first year, I made my own costume with some white pajamas and dishwashing gloves. I bet I looked really strange. By the next year I had some green scrubs, which my mom shortened and pinned up, and a surgical mask. Then came the year I had a real stethoscope, which I found at a yard sale. The last time I went trick-or-treating, I even had wingtip shoes and a doctor's satchel to put my candy in. And fake blood on my outfit.

By the way, doctors on television looked stupid to me, and popular

8

images of doctors had little effect on me. And my own family physician was a boring old clod.

There were some important events that brought the art of surgery to my youthful attention. The first happened when my third grade class took a field trip to the U.S.S. Constitution, the US Navy's oldest commissioned warship. This was the actual ship that had fought in the Revolutionary War. From the dock, she looked immensely tall, with a thousand ropes laced to all the masts and yardarms above. The sides of the ship were thick and high, and were painted black, with a white stripe along the gun ports. We were told that the British cannon balls bounced off her hull during battle. She had a mystical presence, which I could feel quite well, because I was a child, and children are wide open to that stuff.

I remember the strong smells of tar and mildew. The wooden decks were very rough, and the barefoot sailors must have developed great calluses running on it, and climbing the rigging. I could relate— I liked being barefoot. We took a tour guided by a man dressed as a sailor of the eighteenth century, and saw all the nautical equipment that he would have used in action, including the fabulous cannons, which were tied to their gun ports with rope as thick as my arm. We went down a narrow ladder to tour the cramped, dark spaces the sailors lived in, under the main deck. The adults had to stoop to walk under the beams, but at age nine, I could stand up comfortably. We saw the hammocks the sailors slept in, laced like small furled sails between the guns. I felt that I belonged there. Then we got to the surgeon's quarters. It was nothing but a tiny closet with a floor painted red to hide bloodstains. There was a display of antique surgeon's instruments, and they looked like tools of torture. A crescent shaped knife with an ivory handle, and a matching fine toothed saw for amputations. Bits of wire, I don't know what for, pliers, bandages, and cauterizing irons, used to literally sear a wound's blood vessels shut. And a lump of lead wrapped in leather. The tour guide told us that there was no anesthesia in the old days, and when the brandy or rum ran dry, a victim of a wound would literally 'bite the bullet' while being operated upon. I looked very closely, and could see teeth marks in the gnarled lump.

The tour guide said that after an engagement, the amputated limbs would be gathered up and dumped overboard "by the bucket," and when the ship leaned with the wind, salt water and blood washed over the side. My classmates and I groaned and squealed with disgust and delight. The whole effect of the claustrophobic environment and the ghostly vibes of the place made me have internal visions of the nautical surgeon at work, during a battle, with the splinters of wood and steel flying around, and the acrid smoke of the guns; it must have been horrible! Screams and explosions still vibrated in the air around me. In a moment of transcendental reverie, I concluded that of all the jobs on the ship, the surgeon's was the most exciting. He must have been physically strong, possessing dexterous skills, and bravery. He was as highly educated as the Captain, and trusted universally. How could any other person onboard embody such attributes? He must have been a rare and valuable commodity on the high seas, in the hoary days of old. A gambler who could not cheat, a minister who could not promise salvation. A friend, in any uniform, under any flag.

The second event that crystallized my decision to become a surgeon happened when I was in the fifth grade. I received Mary Shelly's book *Frankenstein* for Christmas. It was the present my Aunt Janice the librarian had mailed from Seattle. I had never really cared for the matched volumes of the literary classics she sent me every year for Christmas and my birthdays, and thus had held the package off till last, not knowing what a gem it was to be. Near dawn the next morning, I put down 'The Modern Prometheus,' mesmerized, convinced that the good Doctor's only real problem was not lack of skill or courage or ingenuity, but the general lack of professional legitimacy of the medical trade at the time. I sensed that this Dr. Frankenstein was the type of man who would have been a Naval Surgeon, if he had the opportunity. I reasoned that if Doctor Frankenstein had been able to procure the organs and limbs he needed *legitimately,* then his creation–his 'Race,' as he put it–might have been a success; indeed it would have been a marvelous gift to humanity.

Right away, I began to ponder whether contemporary medical advancements could perhaps render Frankenstein's procedure feasible, and what struck me immediately was that if one were inspired to perform work of such magnitude in our own contemporary age, at least we are blessed to live in a world where the experiment could be performed under the best conditions possible, in an appropriate sterilized setting, with decent subject material, and the chance of a successful outcome would supposedly be thus far greater.

I pondered whether this lofty kind of work would ever be attempted in my lifetime. This was years before genetic cloning, a similarly ambitious concept that is now commonly discussed in ethical and clinical terms.

So I became very interested in surgery, and over the following years, I allowed myself to become drunken with dreams of prestige. Not fame, as a football player or rock star might acquire. I wanted celebrity as a *surgeon*. It feels strange to admit it out loud, but I even dreamed of winning the Nobel Prize. I began to read everything I could find in my school library about surgery, and I had my luckiest break ever when I was in the seventh grade. I was usually picked on by some of the neighborhood bullies on my way home from school, so I took shortcuts through back streets and alleys to avoid them. One day I was exploring my very favorite alley, looting the waste bins behind the bookstores on Adams Avenue, and I found a crate of discarded medical textbooks. Some of them were very old. I lugged the entire box home. After the thrill of looking at the wretched illustrations was over, I began to read them. Many of the procedures, mending of the cleft palette, lifting the cataract from the eye, turned out to be very old operations.

I was already aware of the medicine practiced by the colonial Americans, but I tried to imagine these delicate operations being performed at a time even more remote. The dangerous proscribed bleedings, the leeches, the cauterizing of wounds, it was more gruesome than all the horror movies in the world, but it had been real, and instead of being gratuitous, these historical accounts of surgery amazed me with the almost brazen attempts of our ancestors to cure themselves with such vague knowledge, and such crude tools! I discovered in these faded volumes a vast and inescapable challenge: To join the great pioneers of surgery, the classics such as Galen and Hippocrates, the anonymous barber surgeons of the medieval period, even the loathed 'Burkers,' the grave robbers of the eighteenth and nineteenth centuries! I longed to become a great surgeon and bring new procedures to the world, to make a name for myself.

Look at the daring work of Jenner, who terrified Europe with his radical approach to the Cowpox epidemic. He thought of injecting people with a weakened sample of the infecting agent to induce immunity. His detractors printed cartoons of his subjects spontaneously morphing into cows after receiving his treatment, and to this day, we still refer to immunizing injections as vaccinations, a word that literally means: "to make like a cow"!

Consider Roentgen, the discoverer of the use of x-rays in medicine. The first x-ray of a human patient was of a hunter's hand that had been sprayed with shotgun pellets, and there, suspended in the ghostly image of the hand and its skeleton, are the little white dots that showed the surgeon where every single pellet, and every broken bone was. Could we imagine modern medicine without his discovery?

I know it seems naive to claim to want so much, but I felt inspired by the contributions of the masters of the past. My passion, my calling, had been born. Over the years, I have developed more and more elaborate rationalizations for my glorified attitude towards surgery and medicine.

I will share only the main one with you here, the one that persists, in spite of all that I have recently witnessed: it is that while the history of our civilization can be read in great literature, viewed in artworks, and heard in music; the hallowed history of medicine and surgery is not a subjective experience. It is one that we all carry around *within* the object of our very bodies. The benefit of medical science is not an invisible figment of the mind, like the memory of a favorite song, it is an ever present fact, like a bridge or a building; but instead of being merely useful, the physician's gifts are necessary for life to be lived: an arm that was broken and reset, or a leg that was saved from infection. Can a man prove that he is better for having gazed upon the work of Vermeer, or for having listened to a Bach fugue? He can claim to be edified, assuaged... but can this art consumer prove empirically his degree of improvement, or demonstrate his vital dependency upon a work of art? Of course not!

The art lover is reduced to claims of vague internal feelings, which can never be quantified or verified, no matter how emphatically they are stated. Yet an appendectomy or even a tracheotomy could save his life– in a matter of moments! The Caesarian section was actually developed before the time of Julius Caesar, whose dangerous birth gave the operation its very name, and it is still performed, but now, due to constant improvement, it saves the lives of mothers as well as their children. Clearly, of all the ancient arts, those of the surgeon are the most necessary. A painter who is too sick to paint may as well be blind. He may as well be dead. He needs the doctor more than the doctor needs him.

My obsession with surgical procedures lasted through my excruciatingly lonely adolescence and into my adulthood, and finally into my career as a research scientist. Of course, by this time, I had sublimated my childish hopes of personal fame, and those petty and selfish concerns had gradually been replaced by a total focus on my work, and the progress of those patients under my care. And so I may have continued forever as an acolyte at the altar of medicine, working with blind reverence and devotion.

Then I became involved with another doctor's experiment, and a series of events occurred that completely uprooted all of my unexamined self-conceptions, and forced me to see how dangerous my skills had become, in the hands of one as unaware and malleable as I. Unfortunately, that project is not a secret any longer, and it has developed a life of its own, a life that I now wish to end. I was there when this project made the irreversible transit from the merely feasible to the potentially criminal. To the immoral. I watched in horror as it escaped its intended outcome and grew like a cancer. I still try to accept the fact that the project is now out of my control, being co-opted by the men in black, the crop circle artists, and the pharmaceutical industry. But it doesn't matter. They won't get it right either.

And now I have been called upon by my wife and my newfound moral consciousness to recount the deeds I committed while under the influence of my obsession, at the expense of what any rational person would call propriety. May God, or at least my victims, or any of you countless future victims of this unholy blight on the face of history, forgive me.

Chapter 2: My Education

So I was what you might call a "typical" child prodigy. Drunk with the desire to become a doctor as soon as possible, I studied hard in school, and with my parents' consent, I skipped two grades. I guess I never really developed a life, a social life, the way other "normal" teenagers do. I simply studied. I knew that the academic competition at the pre-med level was fierce. Medical students have been known to commit suicide near test time. At my college, the hopeless ones jumped into the bicycle racks below the tallest building, to be extra sure. I overheard someone saying that it seemed unfair to the owners of the damaged bikes. I forced myself to excel in all my classes, even the ones that seemed unrelated to medicine, things like literature, art, mandatory electives, which I tolerated begrudgingly. I never attended any of the school dances. I was younger than everyone around me, and I managed to have things to study on all the important social nights.

It is not as if I did not want to date. My overwhelming concept of the entire female gender was such a vast and unfathomable feature of reality that I simply decided to ignore it. Looking back, I can remember older girls teasing me, making lewd comments that embarrassed me. I tried to ignore them, and I tried to ignore my own curiosity for female companionship. There was no one my age to date! And even if there were people there my age, how could they possibly understand me? I was driven. I had priorities! I promised myself that I would begin dating as an adult, after I got my degree, when I would be free to approach the 51 percent majority of the population of our planet with the same clarity that I brought to bear upon my studies. Besides, I had read all about females in my books, and I was aware that to pursue the females around me while drunk on adolescent hormones would expose me to the kind of humiliating situations that all teenagers unwittingly subject themselves to. I determined that I could postpone all of my romantic aspirations until I was capable of approaching them with the sober awareness and the confidence of an accomplished professional adult. I actually thought that having a medical degree would even solve all of life's romantic problems. So by keeping myself chaste as a monk, by subverting my repressed desires into pure learning energy, I made it into a great college at a very young age.

I was sixteen.

I was compared by an old doctor form Britain to some young man who was the "Youngest Pilot in the R. A. F." Which must have been meant as a great compliment. At first I felt strange around the older students, but everyone around me was too busy to talk, even with each other. Everyone was obsessed with medicine, and for the first time in my life I felt normal. I enjoyed my undergraduate years and kept my GPA in the high 390's, but I could not seem to resolve the central question of exactly what kind of surgery I was going to specialize in.

That decision was something else that I had postponed. Trauma always appealed to me because it is exciting and especially relevant to today's violent culture. Heart surgery has a symbolic majesty to it, and the technology of the field is incredibly sophisticated. I even considered the veterinary sciences, because it seems so tricky to have to diagnose such a wide variety of patients entirely from examination, without being able to discuss the ailment verbally (paradoxically, I later decided that this would possibly make it easier). Until then, I had never used an animal as a test subject in an experiment. Looking back, I see that what I was looking for was not a calling, but a hero, someone who was trying to solve a problem that intrigued me, in a compelling way. A modern Galen or Jenner. I guess I am fortunate that I was in this way able to hold onto some of my original childhood optimism, which so many of my fellow medical students seem to lose on their way to becoming doctors.

I found my hero after receiving my Master's degree. His name was Dr. Arthur Cook, the celebrated nerve specialist, who began his career with a major development in the realm of hand surgery. I read an article about him in *American Microsurgery Quarterly*. There was an interview with this man who had pioneered the use of a computer controlled robotic arm in microsurgery, and a photograph of him riding what appeared to be a vintage Triumph motorcycle, wearing goggles and a Harris tweed jacket, with a puff of gray smoke following the bike. At that time helmets were not mandatory in North Carolina. In the photo, he waved at the camera. I sensed the irony of a genius like him risking his precious brain for a little fun on a sunny day. I actually had an old motorcycle myself.

He had the grin of someone who was doing what he enjoyed. Dr. Cook's latest development was a camera-equipped laser with an articulated, remote-controlled mount. It could be used as a scalpel or as a cauterizing unit, and was normally clamped onto a 'halo,' which is a strong but very light carbon-fiber ring that bolts onto the patient's cranium. Arthur claimed that with his equipment, a doctor could do work more delicate than ever before, even from remote locations, via the internet. This latest idea has only recently become widely available.

When I sent my application to his lab, I was aware that he might have had other fans with better resumes than mine, so I decided to travel to the city where he lived, and literally camp outside his doorstep, like a rock-and-roll groupie. I stated in my very polite cover letter that I would be in the area for the summer and would like a chance to meet him, at his convenience. He caught me off guard by calling me first. He told me we could both save some time and do the interview, "right now, over the phone."

For a moment I was nervous to the point of muteness, but right then, something inside me clicked, and I spontaneously paraphrased my resume, more or less in its entirety, from memory. It had been excruciating in the writing, but I could actually hear myself talking, and I have to admit, I was astounded at my own memory of it in the moment. I listed my major academic achievements, I told him who my favorite instructors were, what extracurricular hospital projects I was involved with, and why I was eager to work with him specifically. I told him that I read his article in *AMQ*. He listened silently to my rapid soliloquy. He then said "Hmmm," and something to the effect that my near-perfect GPA was "average," and he asked me if I had any special interests or hobbies other than developing my *medical career*, which he pronounced as if he were exhaling as he said the words. I realized that I had nothing in my resume about non-medical interests. I panicked.

I closed my eyes and said, "I heard you like old motorcycles, sir."

He politely asked if I rode a 'cycle.

"Yes, I ride a Gilera Saturno."

"One of the new ones?"

"No, it's a '58, a *real* Gilera Saturno."

"Where did you get such a bike?"

"My uncle brought it home in boxes from Italy in the early sixties, when he was in the army."

"Who put it back together?"

"I did. It took a while."

"Oh... well I think I'd like to take a ride on that."

"Well then you'd better know how to bump-start a bike, because it has no kick lever!" We laughed.

We discussed motorcycles for a while, then he began telling me about his latest project.

As I listened, my heart was literally pounding.

"Victor, the future of surgery is going to be changing soon, and my current research may someday make most of your education completely irrelevant. If you want to use what you know forever then don't bother me. If you want to be part of this new generation of technology, well, I'd really like your help."

I gladly accepted. I was inspired by the very sound of his voice. He sounded like an American Sean Connery. We got along famously, and he taught me everything I know about the repair of nerve tissue under the microscope, including the use of the computer-controlled laser, or 'the Machine' as he called it.

Arthur also collected and restored old motorcycles, single cylinder models especially, like the Saturno of mine, which he said was "the only real bike the Italians ever made." Under his guidance I also became a reasonably good mechanic and we spent afternoons in his garage tinkering with old engines, using smudged yellow-paged manuals and obsolete Whitworth wrenches.

Up till that time, I had always felt guilty about spending time doing anything other than homework. He would speak softly to a bike while he worked on it. And curse. Cook believed that the only way to solve the great problems in life was to know when to leave them and play for a while. This concept was new to me. His other great technique for solving problems seemed to be taking a nap and waking up with the answer. I still struggle to master this second talent.

Soon after I started at the new school, Cook's wife invited me over for dinner. Lillian collected Chinese snuff bottles. These are tiny bottles of glass or carved quartz. They are only about two inches tall, and many have small pictures painted inside them. She told me the story of the snuff bottle painters, who painted while lying on their backs, looking up through the glass. They used paintbrushes made with a single eyelash, laying each stroke between breaths.

"She should have been a surgeon," Arthur said.

When we first met, Lillian asked me how old I was. She looked at me as if I was a kid. After she got to know me better, she asked me if I was gay. I was startled, and Cook said "Lillian!"

"Well, you don't have a girlfriend, Victor, and you seem to know very little about dating."

"He doesn't go on dates!" said Cook. "He's a serious student!"

Lillian asked me if I wanted her to fix me up on a date. Before I could answer, Cook stepped in and told his wife that I would date all the young ladies she knew after our research paper was completed. We all looked at each other and I said, "Yes, Lillian, I promise."

This sweet old couple became like second parents to me, and

Lillian did eventually fix me up with a series of girls who seemed hopelessly unsuited to me. Most of them were older than me. She opined that my uncle had given me the old motorcycle to "chase the girls." I told her that he had actually had planned on racing it, but that he became a father and did not feel like risking his neck any longer.

Dr. Cook's new medical investigation involved using various hormones and proteins that spiders secrete in their venom to aid the process of grafting flatworms back together after they had been frozen and cracked into halves. Muscle and nerve cells are not naturally replaced by the body, as are skin or blood cells. That makes them difficult to repair. But Arthur had access to a mysterious source of potent new drugs that we tested which allowed severed nerves and certain muscles to heal very quickly, and even regenerate. I felt the ultimate high—the feeling that what we were doing could really improve the surgeons' craft, save lives, and make life worth living for people who, if not for our work, would suffer. Secondarily, I felt the rush of excitement associated with avant-garde science. There is academic and social acclaim, and millions of dollars to be made in the medical industry, and there is no use in denying that.

I felt the thrill of being among the first to see the effects of a new process that seemed to work miracles. Then Arthur Cook passed away in the fall of last year. He died suddenly, and Lillian was holding his hands. She saw me crying and said "don't worry Victor, it's not your fault." She knew that I was blaming myself for not taking better care of him. After all, I was practically a doctor! I had been so busy watching damaged material heal itself under the microscope that I had been unaware of my best friend's declining general condition, right next to me. How could I have missed it? Had he hidden his deteriorating health from me, and if so, why? I was despondent for a while, but Lillian told me that she had been encouraging Arthur to work after most men his age retire "so that he could die happy."

For a few days, I was paralyzed with anger at the notion that the human body is perfect in so many ways, but that it seems bent on self-destruction. Soon my resolve to complete Dr. Cook's research returned, and I finished our paper: *The use of Arachnid-derived Anticoagulant Enzymes and Proteins in Nerve Tissue Repair in Flatworms.* It did receive a lot of positive response in the medical journals, and we received some money from a consortium of investors in Texas to continue the project, but our names obviously have not become household words. I dedicated the paper and my career to Dr. Cook's memory.

Chapter 3: Meet Elvin Williams

I continued on as head of the laboratory. The students working in the lab were as somber as I was, but we were all friends, and that helped. Some of us developed a process manual for 'the Machine.' The rest of us worked on perfecting the enzyme process, and initiated the FDA testing protocol.

One day, I received a handwritten fax claiming to be from Elvin Williams, the pharmaceuticals tycoon known in the medical establishment as "the King." This letter seemed so absurd that I carried it around in the pocket of my lab coat, showing it to my friends at the institute, trying to figure out who was pulling the prank. By lunchtime the general consensus of my colleagues was that this thing was bona fide original. I was eating in the cafeteria and I took it out of my pocket and read it again as I ate. Here is what it said:

"Dear Victor:

I must ask that you participate in a special project that I cannot discuss in this note. I am aware that you are conducting important research begun by the late Dr. Cook. He and I were business partners and friends, and I hope that I do not sound impertinent when I state that our priorities demand your special skills here. I am prepared to compensate you at a premium level for your considerable expertise, and for the short notice of my request. If you honor the memory of Dr. Cook, then you will contact me as soon as possible…

…Elvin Williams"

The reason that I had initially thought the thing was a fake (besides its pompous tone) was that it was handwritten. When I re-read it through again, the handwriting appeared to be unaffected, and his signature looked friendly. The first letters of his name were large, but all the following letters were clear. Although his handwriting was pretty, it was not embellished, it was simply old-fashioned looking. I went to my office cubicle and called the long distance number in the letter, wondering if I was a great ass falling for someone's practical joke. I took a quick look at the people around me. No one was looking at me. The phone rang once and was answered by a very old man. Although I had never heard Dr. Williams speak, I realized that this was the King himself, and I sat down.

"Good morning Victor, thank you for calling me. Are you very busy for the next month or two?"

It was not really true, but I said no.

He told me there would be a ticket reservation for me at the airport, where I would fly to San Diego, and that a driver would deliver me to the Veteran's Hospital in La Jolla, where he was.

I asked him why he was in the hospital.

He was silent, then he actually said, "Oh, I just need to have my aortic valve rebuilt."

I digested this news.

Then he asked, "Do you know anything about the Yucatan peninsula?"

I hesitated, and said no.

He recommended a few titles, including a recent edition of *Yucatan Anthropology*.

"It will be a long flight, get my *Annotated Pharmacopoeia of Southern Mexico...* anything you could find about the Indians of the Yucatan would help. Do you speak Spanish?"

I answered no for the third time, and I then asked him, as politely as I could, what this was all about.

"Victor, I have discovered, in the jungles of southern Mexico, something that I have searched for all my life, something that I need to have you retrieve for me."

23

I was silent.

"So, do you want in?"

'In...to what?' I thought to myself. Fortunately, I heard myself quickly saying: "Yes! Of course I will help, Dr. Williams, any friend of Cook's is a friend of mine."

I took down the reservation details and he said goodbye. I hung up the phone, literally speechless, and I was even motionless for a moment. I described the vague details of my situation to my student-assistants as best I could, and gave them the task of maintaining our projects. Then I got out my doctors' bag. We surgeons do still own those things, at least I do, and I am proud of it. Lillian Cook gave me this one as a graduation present, so I will describe it.

It is a Holmes-Sutton Royal Instrument Attaché, with internal compartments and a lift -out tray for small items. It has my initials embossed over the clasp in gold, and a combination lock latch, and an embroidered badge inside it stating that it was made "by Appointment to Her Royal Majesties' Medical College of Doctors & Physicians," et cetera. It smells good inside. I tried to imagine what a traveling surgeon might need, presumably in the Yucatan jungle. Of course, I could not take the laser machine and halo with me, but I do have many special tools used just for neuro-surgery, I got them all in with little room to spare.

I also carry a less attractive fisherman's tackle box. It is orange plastic, and says 'Fish Pal' on the side. It is stuffed with gloves, suture sets, dressings, intubation gear, syringes and sharps, bags of Ringer's lactate, that EMT kind of stuff.

On the way out of school I stopped by the library and photocopied a few articles about the Yucatan, and picked up two of the books Elvin mentioned.

I went home and began to read. I studied the geography of the flat plain that the jungle sits on. I read about the people that inhabit the forest. I read about the insects that thrive in the bed of rotting leaves that pads the forest floor, the insects that bore into the tree trunks and float in the air and the insects that are born and live in the canopy of leaves above, touching the ground only in death, sometimes not even then. I fell asleep. When I woke up I packed a suitcase.

I gave my cat's dish, cat food and twenty dollars to the little old lady across the hall. Mrs. Pruett, feeds my cat when he visits her, and she usually had Tux, as she calls him, over there in her apartment. I think my cat figured out how to go out my window and around the side of the building to hers. Mrs. Pruett, had already bought a covered litter box, a matching scoop, and scented sand not too long before. My cat was asleep on the top of her refrigerator and would not come down to say goodbye to me. Mrs. Pruett, told me that Tux would probably be glad to see me when I got home. When she asked where I was going, I told her "I don't know... San Diego for sure, then maybe somewhere in Mexico." When I looked at her, I sensed that Mrs. Pruett, felt a bewildered pity for me. I smiled and told her not to worry, that I would be home soon. Her look became even more worried, and she reached up to Tux, who rubbed his face against her hand and purred.

As I flew to San Diego, I read the articles in the magazines Elvin had recommended. According to one author, the northeastern corner of the Yucatan peninsula had been the last hiding place of the descendants of the ancient Mayans. They retreated further and further into the thick jungle to escape the Aztecs, and then the Spaniards. The cities of the Yucatan civilizations are only now being discovered. In one magazine there was a feature about an expedition consisting of an anthropologist, a botanist and a biologist working in the forest. It looked like there were no stone structures to study, but there were great photographs of the natives. These distant relatives of the Mayans were small and had round faces, flat noses, and almond - shaped eyes. They looked like Persian cats. Their priests could still read the ancient hieroglyphics and they used a version of the old circular calendar, although they no longer called themselves Mayans. They are the Yohimbe.

Toward the end of the article, I learned that the expedition was funded not by a pharmaceutical company, but by Dr. Williams himself. I had also found an interview with "Elvin Williams, the KING of herbal medicine" in a holistic health journal. Apparently he was one of the first entrepreneurs in the herbal medicine trade, and he is considered the foremost specialist in the botanical cornucopia of the Yucatan jungle. He got his nickname because in the starched world of pharmaceuticals, he dressed outrageously, his deep voice also made him sound sort of like Elvis, and his name was similar. In the early fifties he had discovered a variety of plant, which is used in the manufacture of a major heart medicine. The discovery made the drug much more efficacious, and that began what turned out to be an amazing series of new discoveries. He has apparently saved millions of lives. I learned that Elvin was one of the few figures in the pharmaceutical industry who knew his way around in the "New Age" herbal medicine market as well, and he went out of his way to build a bridge between conventional medicine and the alternative systems. He developed the concept of seeing a continuum of medicine, from the exotic potions of chanting sages, through the conventional allopathic medicine to the mundane and pedestrian cures of simple "healthy living." For him, everything from chemotherapy to ginseng and chicken soup has a place on this one spectrum of healing products. And while some of his conventional science colleagues may have sneered behind his back, he frustrates his critics by being a successful scientist. It was also clear from my reading that when Elvin was on an expedition, he worked very closely with the native people that he met. He interviewed locals in their own dialect, paying his informers with machetes, vegetable seeds, cash, bright red lipstick, or "anything else they wanted, except guns."

He learned which leaves or insects were used by local healers. Then he collected samples, working under the sun, in makeshift laboratories. He had an intensely magnetic personality that caused people to want to help him. In his lab in California, his staff would isolate the active ingredient, if it really existed, and test the drug against conventional alternatives, if they existed. He tested many drugs on himself, and once when he suffered a broken arm, he had a special extract injected into the site, and kept progress reports, leading to an entirely new class of drugs. He would then develop programs for harvesting the ingredients in an ecologically sound fashion, and was thus popular with environmentalists at home, and the local politicians, who saw the natives get work gathering the material from the forest themselves. The King was also famous for the dangerous habit of traveling deep into the jungle alone, with minimal gear, paddling an old green camouflaged fiberglass canoe up the countless and ever-changing rivers of the forest. He spoke Spanish as well as several jungle dialects.

My brief study of the man, as it appeared to me after a few hours reading, was that Elvin was obsessed with the jungle and its inhabitants as I had been with surgery as a child. He was quoted as saying: "It is only natural for us to be afraid of the jungle, because it seems alien to our urban sensibilities, but we all are the children of the warm, green, food-filled forest, the womb of humankind itself."

It was late, and as I fell asleep, I imagined the 'warm, green, forest,' stretching into the distance forever.

Chapter 4: San Diego

A stewardess woke me up and asked me to fasten my seatbelt. I looked out the window at the pale blue swimming pools in the backyards below. Does everyone in Southern California have a swimming pool? People's voices were dim, and I watched the cars crawling along as we landed in the middle of the city. In the center of the city. As I looked out the window, the houses and buildings rushed by, and as we sank into the runway, we passed over a hill and swept down just over people's rooftops. I wondered why the San Diegans did not locate their airport somewhere else.

A driver was waiting for me with my name on a card as I exited the ramp in the airport. That was a first for me, and it made me feel strange. I speculated about the lifestyle of the vastly wealthy, who lived in the beautiful homes I saw as he drove me to the hospital. I maintained a nervous silence in the large passenger compartment, empty except for me. There was a TV set, but at that time I did not watch television.

The veterans' hospital had a patriotic décor. The linoleum floors were shiny, and historic battle scenes were depicted in murals on the walls. Everything seemed very orderly. I got to Elvin's room and looked in. I recognized him from the pictures in the reading material. Elvin's bed was one of six and sat in the corner of a room, which was located in a corner of the hospital, and there was a window to each side of him. The light these windows cast upon him gave him a very luminous appearance, and he had raised his bed to a sitting position, and he had propped himself up with pillows. I had expected to meet him alone, but he had two other elderly gentlemen with him. I tried to hide a sensation of confusion.

Elvin looked at me with a warm smile and politely thanked me for responding to his summons. He introduced me to his companions, Pat and Walter. Pat was closest to me, in a wheelchair. He wore a blue baseball cap with gold leaves embroidered on the bill and an eagle insignia on the front. Walter was a handsome fellow with dark skin and a thin mustache. He sat in a regular chair, opposite Pat and I, with his back to the window. The men had pulled rolling tables up over Elvin's lap, and had dealt out cards for a game. Each man had a handful of tongue depressors in his shirt pocket. Pat offered me a chair next to him. We all shook hands, and I sat down. We all looked at Elvin. Elvin broke the ice by mentioning to me that he had hoped to get Arthur Cook himself to help him, but as we both knew, Cook had recently passed away. He looked down and we were all silent for a moment.

He broke the silence. "Arthur told me you would be perfect for this job."

Elvin explained to me that he had met Arthur years ago and had corresponded with him regularly, but I could not recall Arthur ever mentioning Williams to me.

"I supplied the serum that you were using in the flatworm nerve-grafting experiment."

"What the heck was that stuff?" I asked. "It's a miracle!"

"Oh, that was just one of the many gifts that I received from our generous friends, the Yohimbe. So you see, Victor, you've been working with me for a while now already."

If it were possible, I became even more interested in Dr Williams.

Pat asked me if I played poker.

"Sorry, sir, I've never learned how to gamble."

"Not even in school?" Elvin asked as he scooped some tongue depressors out of a box and handed them to me.

"That's fifty dollars worth."

Wally got an envelope out of his pocket, and began writing on the back. We all watched.

"Here you go. Just bet more if you have something from the middle of the list or better."

I read the list, and jotted down a clarification or two. So a full house is 3 and 2 of a kind. I did not know that. Pat dealt the cards, and we all looked at what we had. I had a pair, and I asked for three more and got a full house. Excellent! It was quiet while everyone evaluated his cards, then Elvin began to tell a long story.

"I was a twenty-year-old medical corpsman in the Navy. We (he gestured to his companions) had been ordered to destroy a German submarine. He had been taking pot shots at shipping off the approaches to the Panama Canal. We spotted him and we got lucky, because for some reason, the German could not submerge below periscope depth, but he fled north at a fast pace, and we almost lost him a few times. We chased him all the way to the southern coast of Mexico, where we deployed in the smaller PT boat and pursued the U-boat into a river delta. It was a beautiful day, and we were creeping around these tiny islands, all hands manning the deck guns, hoping to catch him in the open.

"On the second day up the river, we found a native paddling a canoe that was full of food. Food is one thing sailors always need more of."

Pat and Wally nodded.

"The native had fish, bananas, pineapples, mangoes, papayas, coconuts, combs of honey in a basket, and even a wild boar, trussed to a tree branch, and bound tight. Wally, here, speaks Spanish."

I looked at Wally

"Hola!" he said with a smile.

"We called him topside to see if he could talk with this Indian. As it turned out, the native was the only person in his tribe who could speak Spanish. His name was Atay, and he was traveling to a city about twenty miles down the coast to trade the food for supplies. Salinas did a great job haggling and we got the whole boatload of food for the fire axe, a shovel, a coil of heavy rope, a canteen and some rubber hose and empty pop bottles. That afternoon we ate a huge feast, on the deck of the boat. The Indian told Salinas that all the deep water was behind us, but he admitted that there were many other branches of the delta, and that the U-boat could be anywhere. We decided to drop anchor for the night, because it was getting dark. We all had chores to do around the boat. It is normal for a boat to take on a small amount of water, which had to be occasionally pumped overboard. Mr. Salinas uncovered and primed the bilge pump, a single cylinder engine mounted temporarily on the deck. Unfortunately, Wally's hand was near the belt pulley as he started the motor. The pump rumbled to life, and sucked his hand between the belt and pulley, crushing it terribly. He fell away from the pump screaming in agony. The injury was severe and I administered morphine out of the first aid kit, applied a tourniquet just below the elbow, and dressed the wound. I was worried, because Pat here, who was a lowly Lieutenant, junior grade, at the time, told me that it would take at least a day to get back to the ship, after we finished looking for the German. I told him that the longer it took, the higher the chances were that the doctors on the ship would amputate Wally's hand. Salinas heard us talking about it. Even though he was pretty drowsy from the sedative, he began shouting. Atay wanted to know what was going on. Salinas told Atay that we were going to cut off his hand."

Elvin stopped telling the story and noted that it was time for us to show our cards. I won. I gained ten tongue depressors.

Pat dealt another hand. I think we played about six hands as Elvin spoke, and I enjoyed listening while I played.

"So the native, Atay, told Wally that he could take him to his Chief, a great doctor named Eight Jaguar, who had powerful medicine, and could save his hand. We all listened as Wally translated, and Atay showed us a scar on his leg. He explained to us that he had been crushed under a fallen tree, and that his Chief fixed him. Indeed, there was a long scar on his leg, surrounded by puncture wounds, and all had been neatly closed with tiny suture marks."

I began to find it difficult to concentrate on the game at this point.

"This had been a compound fracture. We discussed the witch doctor idea. Salinas actually wanted to go with the native; he told us he would go even if they were cannibals! I was experiencing a powerful curiosity about this witch doctor and his medicine. Wally reasoned that if he was going to lose his hand anyway, then it could not matter what the 'Indios' did. "I decided on the spot that this was one of those moments in life that requires decisive action. I took Pat aside and tried to reason with him: 'You went to college, you know what something like this could be worth to the war effort!'"

"And he was right!" said Pat, betting a big pile of tongue depressors.

"The Lieutenant told Wally to explain to Atay that if anything were to 'happen' to us, that they could keep our possessions, and even our heads, but must leave the dog-tags on our bodies, or our spirits would haunt them! I really liked that. We tried not to laugh. Wally translated from his stretcher and Atay smiled and nodded when we showed him that all of us wore the tags. Atay and I got into the canoe, and I steadied the boat as the crew lowered Wally over the side. The canoe itself was of amazing construction, and appeared to be made of woven mats of reed sewn over a collapsible wooden frame. The whole thing probably only weighed ten pounds, yet it supported all the trade goods, Atay, Wally, and me comfortably. I looked at the crew and our commander as Atay pushed off and paddled the canoe away. Pat yelled out to me 'what the hell am I doing?' And I hollered back to him, 'we're making the greatest medical discovery of our time!' I know it seems crazy now, but hey– we were all just kids– not one of us was over twenty-five years old! We paddled into the forest, and the space over our heads closed in as we slipped under the branches. The jungle crept up to the sides of the boat and brushed against our elbows as we paddled up the narrow river. It went like that for a while, then the waterway opened up again and the river was wide and there was a small beach, next to a thriving campsite. We had been paddling for an hour. The native people came to the riverbank, pulled the boat up onto the dirt, and surrounded us. So there we were, in the middle of the frikking jungle, surrounded by natives. Atay unloaded the rope, canteens, hose and the axe, and the natives passed them around, and inspected them. Then a gnarly old guy showed up, and everyone stepped away. The old man looked at Wally and me with extreme disdain. He looked at us with an almost wild hatred. He pointed at us and shouted something at Atay. Atay unwrapped the wound on Salinas' hand, and the Chief bent down and looked at it."

At this point Wally lifted his hand from his lap and placed it on the table. We all looked at it. Wally's hand was indeed still marked with a pair of branching scars, right across the palm, but there was also swelling and discoloration in the area, and Wally slowly lowered it to the table. He looked at me and saw my amazement. He smiled and winked at me. I was curious about his condition.

"How much use do you have of your hand, Wally?"

"Well not much, anymore. But it was almost completely functional for most of my life. It only began to act up as I got really old, besides, I have arthritis, so it's not so bad. And it was better than a hook!"

"Thank you, Wally," Elvin said.

"Apparently the medicines are prepared with the patient's blood, to achieve a custom-designed, genetically-perfect compound. But with Mr. Salinas, they had to improvise."

Wally and Elvin looked at each other sympathetically

"Well, I could tell that as soon as the Chief saw this wound, he felt compelled to operate. "He removed the tourniquet, and the wound began to bleed badly. Salinas moaned with pain, and the Chief directed me to come over. He looked at my hands, my short fingernails, my watch. Then he took a bag from a string around his neck, opened it, and poured some powder from it into a tube. He leaned close to me, waited till I was inhaling, and blew the stuff into my face. I instantly got a racking headache. I sat down in the mud, and could not speak. My vision became blurry, and I fell into a hypnotic sleep. With my last confused thoughts I was able to be terrified that I would never be able to wake up, that I would never see the PT boat again, or the ship, or my home. I traveled in my dream back to Idaho, and I saw my old father tending farm equipment, I saw the old Navajo man who drinks whiskey from a flask hidden in an oak tree, and I was so sad and I missed everything that I knew".

"We returned the next afternoon. The crew was beginning to really worry. A few others came with us. Atay and Salinas were in one boat, and there was a young woman paddling another, with the Chief, dressed in fantastic clothes, and me, just waking from my sleep. I had only seen the Chief briefly before he put me to sleep. Now I could admire his costume. He had orange paint spots in his black hair and this magnificent cape made of golden yellow feathers. He wore a kilt of spotted leopard fur, and had bands of beads around his ankles and wrists. He wore feathers in his hair, blue and shiny as a new car. There was a spider monkey perched on the prow of the canoe. I was only just coming to, and the crew did not know that I was asleep through the whole thing. I was just as surprised as they were by the miraculous cure of the hand that Salinas held up for us to see. His hand was still swollen and the scars seemed to be dyed black, but his hand was definitely all in one piece, and he could even— just barely—move his fingers.

"I was still light-headed, but I was completely amazed by what I saw. I was not yet an MD, but I knew beyond a shadow of a doubt that I was witnessing a medical impossibility. I inspected the wound closely. There were scalpel marks that radiated away from the wound, implying that the bones in the palm had been worked back into place. There were tiny suture marks around all of the incisions, but the sutures themselves were not there any more, just a row of   tiny black dots on each side of the scar. Salinas explained to me that the Jaguar Man had rubbed some water on his head, and all the pain in his hand vanished immediately, replaced by a racking pain in his skull. The pain became somehow more bearable, and unlike me, he was able to stay awake and watch what the Indians were doing. He told me that the doctor's wives had soaked his hand in hot vats of different liquids and gently massaged it and curled and uncurled his fingers. They somehow worked the crushed bones and loose flaps of skin and tissues back into their original places. They felt the hand and pulled and pressed it back into shape. Then they sutured some of the scar shut with thorns, and wrapped it all in light cloth. They were massaging it the whole time, even as he slept. On the way back, they told him to wash the bandage off in the river. A lot of dead skin came off with it, but then there was his hand, almost as good as new, and still attached to his arm! Salinas had been talking with Atay all the way back to the Patrol Boat, which was easy to find by listening for the motor. He told us that the Chief had come back to exorcise the pump engine, because it was a danger to the jungle people!"

Elvin laughed a happy laugh and told me that in retrospect, it was typical for the Chief to take responsibility for a dangerous new entity in his jungle. He asked me if I was hungry, and told me that the food in the hospital was pretty good. I accepted. He continued his story.

"We all went to the stern of the boat to watch the exorcism of our evil bilge pump. We were all smiling, and some of us were trying not to laugh. The old doctor was having his feathered cape taken off by the woman. Once the cape was off, we all saw an incredible tattoo on his back. It looked like two jagged blue lines that went down the center of his back, like the bill of a saw-tooth shark. There were tiny blue points on either side of the lightning bolt scars. The woman draped the Chief's cape over her arm, and asked Atay to bring the recently bartered canteen with water in it. The doctor sprinkled some of the water on the pump and waved a small pair of bones at it, snapping them together. He chanted a song and snapped the bones for a while longer, then he stopped abruptly. He patted his hand on the pump. He then put his ear up to it, and we crew members actually fell silent, so he could listen! He turned and told Atay that the pump was cold. He complained that the pump was not a living thing, and could not have bit Salinas. 'It was never alive!' he scolded us."

"When the Chief faced us, I looked closely at his skin, his forehead, at the blue line running across his hairline, with tiny dots above and below it. I noticed that the Chief was making eye contact with me. He then leaned back, lowered his eyebrows, and glared at me as if I was a voyeur and he was deeply offended by my curious staring. I had been inspecting the scar on his forehead like a scientist, and studying the way it was connected to the scar on his back, behind his ears. I had been unaware of my rude behavior. I turned away in shame. I blushed involuntarily and felt sick with embarrassment, and I could not for the life of me account for the strength of this reaction. I was used to examining a person with the eyes of a medic, and I think I used this curious scanning effect on him, and in return, the Chief had psyched me out just by looking at me. I do not think anyone else noticed. I knew exactly what he was talking about. I myself look at people with a clinical detachment that may seem cool–as in cold. At that moment, I noticed that the hair on the back of Elvin's arm was raised. It was obvious that he was still "psyched out" by the Chief, all these years later.

"Someone got the pump started, and the natives watched it chugging away with utter nonchalance. They were invited to look overboard, to see how it spat water out the side of the boat. The witch doctor attempted to put a stick in the fan blade and Wally shut off the motor just as it chewed a few slices off the end. Chief Eight Jaguar looked at the stick and then told Salinas that the beast was stuck to the boat and could not have chased him, and that it was his own fault for putting his hand in the 'teeth.' That broke the ice and we all laughed at them both. Salinas gave Eight Jaguar his watch and he gave Atay a bayonet as payment for fixing his hand, and a pen and some paper to Eight Jaguar's wife, who had found it on her own, rummaging through things in the wheelhouse.

"The Chief's wife helped him put his cape back on, and before we could say a decent farewell, they left. I remember watching them paddle back upstream. They slipped back under the shadows of the overhanging trees, then they simply vanished. We weighed anchor and began drifting back down the river. The U-boat must have left or gotten lost forever, because we did not engage it on our way back to sea. We radioed our ship and the next evening we were back aboard in the luxury of space on the destroyer, after a week on the cramped patrol boat. We still had a lot of the exotic fruit with us. Salinas did not want to be questioned by the doctors on the ship about his hand, and Pat was having second thoughts about how he would explain all this to his superiors, so I gladly went along with the story that the marks on his hand were a tattoo. Wally's hand did heal completely, and I guess the whole event was forgotten after the war, but I kept thinking about the witch doctor, the scars on his back, and the scars on Salinas' hand."

At this point, a nurse brought in the food cart, and Elvin was right. Everything was delicious.

Elvin and the last surviving crewmembers of his PT boat were pleasant dinner companions, but I ate quickly, hoping to get back to his story.

Elvin was looking right into my eyes and asked me,

"You are interested in this story aren't you?"

I said, " Yes."

"Do you believe this story?"

"It's so strange that it has to be true."

Pat and Wally nodded as they ate.

"You want to know about the vats of liquid that the witch doctor used to accelerate the healing process, right?"

I cleared my throat, and again, said, "Yes."

He looked at my solar plexus as he spoke.

"Like I said, I had been afraid of the jungle, when Mr. Salinas was not. I guess he was more highly motivated than I to go there; anyway, I determined to overcome this fear, and return to find the tribe in the jungle, to find Eight Jaguar again, and learn all about his powerful medicine. You may not yet appreciate how hard it is to find a reclusive, nomadic tribe under the canopy of a tropical rainforest, but for me, finding them has turned from a passion, to an obsession, to a matter of life and death! "

He had leaned forward as he said this, then he settled back into his cushions.

"I built my fortune on the trips I made into the jungle collecting drugs and herbs, but my secret motivation to go on those journeys was the hope of finding Eight Jaguar and his tribe again, and learning all about his surgery."

"Are you telling me it has taken you all this time to locate his tribe?" I asked.

"No, but I found them only one other time in thirteen trips. I was forty-four years old by then. I was deep in a river when I saw smoke. I paddled as close as I could, and I became discouraged because the smoke smelled like cigarettes. I tried to sneak up on whoever it was, but they seemed to know I was there. They called out to me and greeted me. I was hiding behind a tree. Atay, the one who spoke Spanish, was there. I was jumping up and down with joy, and so was every kid in the camp! I had learned Spanish after the war, when my search for the witch doctor began. I called out to Atay, and he answered, saying they could smell me a long way off. Then he told me not to be afraid. 'We are not the fierce Yanomamo!'

"He later confessed that he was somewhat apologetic that he had ever allowed us to meet him that day in the river. Atay told me that when he brought Salinas and I to Eight Jaguar, the doctors' first inclination was to summarily kill us, but Salinas promised that he and his friends would give them more trade goods if they returned us to our boat, and that we would go away and never come back. Well, I did come back, and they decided to let me live, and I was finally able to get what I wanted. My theory about the connection between the scars on Salinas' hand and the scars on Eight Jaguar's back turned out to be absolutely correct."

I asked him what this "theory" of his was.

He smiled and took a drink of water, and shifted his weight in the bed. He maintained eye contact with me as he paused, and leaned forward.

"Victor, all of the great and powerful doctors of the Yucatan use plant extracts and spider and snake venom to heal scars, or to have visions, or to kill enemies, which is common stock in trade anywhere in the world. But when a special Yohimbe tribe member gets old, he is given a new body by his apprentices in an amazing operation they call the *Incarnación*."

Here Elvin leaned back and folded his arms across his chest.

I slowly asked Mr. Williams, "a new body?"

Elvin nodded his head.

"The Chief was amazingly candid. Once I got the old bugger to talk, he simply would not shut up! He described the whole thing to me, and even had some documents written in hieroglyphics to help explain the process, although they did not really clarify anything for me and I did not have a working camera with me at the time. His apprentices actually perform this incredible procedure on the aged doctor—talk about a teacher putting faith in his students! First, they shave their Chief's head and open the rear of his cranium, using basic trepanation and cutting tools. Then they cut a special incision down the patient's back. This incision has wedge-shaped cuts where the spinal branches leave the trunk cord at each vertebra, at the rib joints. They cut an identical one in the back of the body of a healthy young man who is the 'host.' They then remove and discard the brain and spine from the host body and swab the cavity with venom preparations and plant extracts. Then, working quickly, they remove the old man's brain and spine all in one piece, with a small disc of skull material remaining around the last vertebra. They then insert the old doctors' central nervous system into the body of the host. The base of the spine is mated to the coccyx of the host."

I asked about rejection of the graft, and Elvin stated that only blood relatives are chosen, and that they have various tests for compatibility and even a system for gradually acclimating the two bodies by using transfusions before the operation.

"How are these wounds closed?" I asked.

"They suture the incision shut with thorns in some places, and the heads of ants. These are large ants, and are held up to the wound site. Their mandibles clamp the scar shut, and the thorax is pinched off. The head remains, and maintains its grip for a day, and by then the patient has recovered."

The card game had been picked up after dinner, but it was going slowly as we listened to Elvin.

"They have developed a very special set of tools to use in the operation, including a special pit to do the operation in. They call it 'the womb'! It is a pit dug in the ground in a special place where there is blue clay. The pit is filled with water and plant juices, which, to the Yohimbe men, represents the amniotic fluid of the womb. They put a tube down the Chief's throat and submerge him in the solution. They put hot rocks into the pit to raise the temperature. They blow into the tube so the patient can breathe. There is a lot of blood, but they say that if they are favored by the Gods, the heart never actually stops beating during the operation. That is how the wisdom of the old witch doctor can stay alive for generations. The members of the tribe revere Eight Jaguar as their God, and his knowledge is truly monumental. In his head lies their entire history, all of their most valuable secrets…"

"I can tell that you are having trouble digesting all this, but I need you to pull yourself together and decide if you want in, right now. We don't have time for the FDA approval or more research. I need you to leave for Mexico tonight, and see this operation for yourself. I need you to go into the jungle and learn the secret of the Incarnación. Eight Jaguar has agreed to let you observe and participate. Then you must return to perform this miracle for me!"

I looked at Pat and Wally.

"We want it too!" Wally said, smiling.

"Everyone will want it!" Elvin laughed.

We sat in silence for a moment. Elvin seemed to look at my forehead, between my eyes as he spoke, and his voice sounded sad, but his eyes weren't sad.

"Listen Doctor Germaine, I have three people in Mexico right now, waiting for a surgeon that I can trust implicitly. Cook picked you for this work, and so I am stuck with you. If you can't do this thing, then I will go ahead and die naturally, like he did."

He gestured to the bed behind the screen next to him and slowly crossed his arms.

I was still in a state of shock but I was able to assure him that I would try to help him. He told me that the Incarnación was only a few days away.

"Thirty two years, eight weeks and three days ago, Eight Jaguar told me his next Incarnación would happen during a specific transit of Venus. This event will occur in three days. My pharmaceutical laboratories have been working on the plant and animal extracts for many years, and you and Arthur did some really critical work as well. So we can procure or synthesize the various plant and animal extracts used by the Indians, but not the surgical technique. That is where you come in. So go and attend this Incarnación; then come back, and bring this gift to me—to all of us."

He looked me in the eyes, as if I might flinch. I did not.

I was delirious with the magnitude of these revelations, I was out of words and I was out of tongue depressors. Elvin and his friends had won all of them. I stood up and leaned to shake their hands.

"I'll do whatever I can do to help you, gentlemen."

Pat and Wally nodded warmly. Elvin's smile radiated confidence, and, coming from this amazing soul, it felt like a real honor. As I left, I paused to see the man in the next bed. His skin was clammy and he had no pulse.

"Hey, you're right. This guy's dead. How did you know?"

"Well, he announced yesterday that he felt like dying today, after watching MASH."

I told them I would notify the nurse about the dead man on the way out, but they told me not to bother. Pat said not to worry, they would tell the nurse later. "We want to finish this poker game first, it was his last wish that someone beat Elvin, at least once."

Elvin recommended a specific immunization that I should get for the trip.

"It's the most recent germ cocktail they have."

And that was it. I soon stepped out of the hospital and the sunset was fantastic. A swirly sky of blues and oranges, framed with the silhouettes of palm trees. Suddenly the limousine rolled up and the chauffeur popped out to open a door for me. I decided to sit in the front with him, hoping to chat with him about his boss. As it turned out, the driver had never met the notoriously thrifty millionaire, and was hired out just for the day. He asked me what my business was in Mexico and I had to tell him that I was not at liberty to explain it, and we rode the rest of the way again, in silence.

Chapter 5: Into the Jungle

After another long flight with a transfer in Mexico City that I barely remember, I woke up in southern Mexico. I do not travel often, and this was my first trip outside the United States. I was disoriented by the tropical motif of the wallpaper, and the ringing of the telephone. It was the concierge notifying me that I had an airport reservation at seven and would be picked up at a quarter till. It was six o'clock. I thanked him and ordered breakfast. Right around that time room service delivered my breakfast, I realized that a major issue concerning this mission had not been addressed during my interview with Elvin Williams.

He had told me that the Incarnación involved the transfer of the spine and brain of Eight Jaguar into a 'host body.' But who was Elvin expecting to be the host for the operation he was anticipating for himself? According to his account of the Yohimbe Incarnación process, it would have to be a relative…I was so absorbed with this mystery that I was in a sort of stupor, and could barely eat. I was stunned that I had not thought to ask Elvin this question when I was talking with him. I was still in this confused state of mind when I arrived at the airport.

I was soon to have more immediate concerns, however, for not only was I to be delivered with other supplies to my final destination in the jungle by helicopter, which was a novel experience, but the pilot had told me that I was to be "dropped into the forest," after the supplies we were bringing had been "dropped." He seemed to think I was used to this sort of thing, and he walked away.

The helicopter had a boom and winch on the side of it and a few men used it to wrestle some crates into the cargo bay. The pilot

43

returned with a helmet and a harness, which he helped me put on. "It will be too loud to talk once we are under way, so I'll explain the sequence to you here. Your expedition is in some very dense forest, and the jungle people do not want to cut a clearing in the trees. The system for dropping supplies into the jungle was developed by the Indians. The expedition is expecting a rendezvous in two hours. We will travel in their general direction, following a radio signal. They will then open a large nylon parachute between the treetops. You will be lowered onto this sheet. The Indians will then lower you the rest of the way to the ground. Would you like a drink before we go?"

I agreed. I had never considered myself the bungee jumper type of guy, and was quickly becoming unnerved by the prospect of having to learn so soon. We walked to the bar, and my new friend recommended a margarita made with Mescal. I had no idea what Mescal was, but it sounded good, and I was trying to get into the spirit of the adventure. As the bartender poured the liquor, I saw a worm swirling around inside the bottle. I hesitated. Then decided not to be rude. After drinking the large margarita so quickly that I almost passed out with brain-freeze, we were soon cruising along over the forest and its twisting, silver ribbons of river. I used the pilots' binoculars to look at the edge of the forest, where it met the river, and I saw that the trees were tall, and under them was a velvety blackness. I tried to imagine the young sailors meeting the Yohimbe in the jungle, so long ago. Looking down, I sensed that the jungle flowing underneath me had not changed at all. The pilot was pointing through the windshield, way out ahead at a tiny, orange plume of smoke hovering over a finger of jungle that cut between two rivers. My body was just beginning to grow tense when a hand dropped heavily onto my shoulder, startling me completely. It was the winch operator, holding up a large hook. He smiled warmly.

I gave salutations to the pilot, and climbed back to the cargo bay. As I was being prepared to be lowered the winch operator said, "Don't worry, even if you fall off the hook, or if I drop you too fast, their sheet will catch you…besides, you won't have to come back this way, you will be returning in these boats."

He nodded toward two of the crates. I thanked him for the help and then we got the message from the pilot that we were over the drop site. The cargo door shot back and the jungle was seventy feet below us. There was a parachute stretched across the treetops, just as advertised. I could not see the people who held the ropes, but the thin cords attached to the edge of the fabric were tied to about twenty separate ropes, each of which stretched into a tree branch, like a spider web. The helicopter's rotor wash made the tarp undulate as if it were floating on the sea. I nearly vomited. The winch operator pulled me back and laughed at me. "That won't help!" he said, "Here, let's get these crates out."

We connected the winch hook to a crate and lifted it off the floor, then the winch rode outside on the boom, and I watched as the crate descended into the parachute. It seemed to sink into the cloth, and as it disappeared I could see that the winch operator was listening to his headset for the command to pull the cable up. The people below us unfastened the hook on the crate and the cable came up quickly. The parachute slowly returned too, spreading across the treetops like paint as the Indians hauled up the lines. The tricky bit was that the descending cargo would swing like a giant pendulum, so the winch operator had to be able to lower the load into the parachute at exactly the right time. As it turned out, the winch operator seemed to be very good as timing the speed of the winch. The other two crates went easily, yet it was my turn to go and I was still terrified. The hook snapped on my chest and I took a parting look at the winch operator.

He offered a genuine smile and said "Adios."

He pulled the slack out of the cable and I felt it lift me, and was surprised to find the sensation almost comfortable, like being hugged. I momentarily wanted to pull the belts and my wrinkled pants out of my crotch, and adjust myself, but I suddenly rode out of the helicopter cabin and over the forest. I descended, looking up at the winch operators smiling face as he waved. It was difficult to look down because of the belts of the harness right under my chin, but I rotated one time before I could feel the parachute brushing my feet. I was marveling at the panoramic view of the endless horizon of green

45

when the cloth began gathering around me. As I descended through the trees, I could feel the tension on the parachute as the leads were lowered by the people in the trees. I was feeling claustrophobic in my cocoon when I touched solid earth. I was shaking.

A high-pitched voice called out. The parachute then fell all around me and I was draped in a pile of nylon and ropes. People all around me pulled the parachute away and unhooked the cable. After I got my helmet off, my eyes had to adjust to the shade under the canopy of leaves. I could see that I was surrounded by people. I recognized two of the expedition members; one of them had a walkie-talkie and was watching the cable and hook clear the forest canopy. There was also a strong looking middle-aged native. He wore an old bayonet knife, and I marveled at the thought that this could be Eight Jaguar. But he had no tattoo on his back: This must be Atay, and he seemed to be running the show. The population seemed to double as those in the treetops returned to earth, sliding down vines and tree trunks. There were about fifty people in the small clearing, and many more stood on the fallen logs around it. The roar of the helicopter faded away and I felt the native's eyes on me as I looked around. For a moment it was perfectly silent.

I took a moment to pull the seat of my pants out of my butt crack, which felt awkward because everyone was watching me. I had been given a pair of earplugs in the helicopter, but even after removing them, it was still silent. Then the sounds of the jungle began to appear. Screeches, buzzing sounds, birds. I realized that in the helicopter I had enjoyed a constant rush of air. Once my body registered the heat of the jungle, I began to sweat profusely. I took a deep breath. Like inhaling steam. The view from the forest floor was overwhelming. I stood in the center of an empty spot in what appeared to be an endless hall, with a million columns supporting the ceiling of leaves, in all directions, as far as my eyes could see. And I just stood there looking straight up, it was like a stained glass window of every hue of green, yellow, blue, with black branches separating the gem-like panes. The sky shone through and sent down blades of powdery light at a slight angle to the gray and black tree trunks. I gathered my wits and looked back down at the people around me. Some of them were looking up, as if to see what I was looking at.

The Yohimbe are beautiful. I don't know why, but as soon as I was looking into their glassy black eyes, I fell in love with them. They are short, with round little bellies. They had bracelets made of beetles tied around their wrists, feathers in their hair, and painted faces. The favorite color for the face was gray-white for the lower half of the face for men, and red, in pretty designs, for the women. Some of them wore flowers in their hair. The man I recognized as the anthropologist from the National Geographic article stepped forward and we shook hands.

"Hello, you must be Dr. Germain! I'm Mark. Welcome to the site of the Incarnation of the Jaguar Dance. Do you mind if the children touch you?"

He had a monkey climbing all over his head and some kids were hiding behind him, holding his fingers and giggling. The kids looked around Mark at me.

I laughed, "Yes, the kids can touch me."

"They think you are really brave…" Mark said.

I told him to just call me Victor and I quietly stated that the helicopter winch drop was really safe.

"No—it isn't!" Mark laughed, "Yesterday the idiot on the helicopter tried to lower two crates at once, and the load spilled all over the place, in fact, some of the stuff you came with today was to replace it."

I asked if they were using the parachute the day before and he said it was a new idea and yesterday was the first time they had tried it, and the winch operator missed the parachute somehow. Mark had apparently gotten the kids excited by telling them that I was coming the way the cargo did, but that the very loud bird would try not to drop me. Mark could tell that I was upset that my life had been risked without my knowing it, when the other expedition member cut in and introduced himself. He was the biologist, Carl Weatherbee. We shook hands. Carl looked me in the eye and said,

"Well, you've got their respect, which they don't give easily."

I looked at Mark, who turned to Carl and said, "Don't worry Carl, the Yohimbe might respect you completely, but just not be showing it."

Carl said, "Hm."

The kids all took a turn at tugging my clothes and a few old men put their hands out to shake my hands the way Mark and Carl had done, and then walked away looking at their hands. One guy who hadn't shaken hands with me smelled the hand of one who had, as if something on me was now on them. A fellow with blue feathers in his hair shook my hand, and another Yohimbe who would not shake my hand examined his. The crowd was thinning out, heading to another clearing. I asked Mark and Carl about the botanist who was in the expedition.

"Oh she's out collecting White Flowers with the old ladies."

I asked, "She?"

Carl and Mark looked at each other and Carl said, "He doesn't know…"

Mark looked past Carl to me, and told me that Minerva, the botanist was Elvin William's daughter. "And she takes her job very seriously." Carl nodded ominously.

We arrived in the larger clearing where the Indians lived. There was a ring of connected huts. They did not have proper walls, they were mostly thatched roofs with poles holding them up. One native slept in a hammock. The ground under him was covered with mats. The huts were not really divided into separate areas, and the occasional screen partitions seemed to exaggerate the lack of privacy in any one area. People were making baskets, cooking, talking, and living their lives. There were a few dogs, pigs on cords, and chickens running around. I caught myself staring at a mother breastfeeding and felt intrusive, as if I was walking down a street with the power to see into people's houses. I turned away and began watching some men at work in a giant hole in the ground. I realized that they were preparing the pit in which the operation would take place. This pit was right in the middle of the ring of huts, and they had chosen the site directly under a large opening in the canopy of leaves above. I guessed that the operation would take place at noon, when the sun would provide direct light. They had cleared the decaying vegetation and soil away from the clay that was the geologic foundation of this area of the jungle. This clay was a pale gray color with marbled veins of a greenish color running through it. It was very dense and cool to the touch and the trench was larger than a hot tub. The digging was difficult and only a small amount of clay could be removed at a time by hand. There were mats of woven palm fronds around the pit and they were woven so tightly that water beaded on them and had to be swept off. I stared into the pit, trying to brace myself for the operation I was to see the next day. I was still in a shocked state of mind. I began thinking about the ritual and the question returned to me, the really big question of who the donor body would be for Elvin William's operation, and I wondered which of these young men, of these Yohimbe, was willing to give his life for the old shaman. After thinking about it for a while, I resolved to ask Mark about it. The pit was being powdered with a thick coating of tan colored dust by boys who were themselves covered with the dust, and wood was piled into it with birds nests stuffed into the openings, apparently as kindling for a bonfire. Carl approached me and began telling me about the pit. "They come from a really remote region to use this clay."

I asked what "really remote" meant.

Carl proceeded to tell me about the expedition's utterly futile previous attempts at finding the Yohimbe.

"They usually live on a plateau in a mountainous region that is on their reservation, and it is off limits to us. It is virtually unexplored. They have supposedly dismantled parts of their temples and relocated them to places that they could conceal and defend, so our only hope of finding them was in trying to catch them here, in this vast area of the delta. They come here to gather certain critical ingredients for their magic potions, and this delta is where the Incarnación is performed."

Mark and Carl looked at each other and Carl said:

"Tell him about Minerva."

Mark nodded and as Carl drank from a canteen, Mark explained:

"Elvin Williams is sort of a cult hero to us, and we were elated when Minerva approached us with this wacky scheme. The legend that Elvin travels in the jungle alone is a myth. He was planning a solo expedition into the Yucatan in the late fifties. His wife Margaret was a war correspondent who was killed in Korea. Elvin decided to enroll their daughter Minerva in a Catholic boarding school in Belize, which is south of here. Elvin and Minerva arrived at the school, and before they even stepped into the compound, the Mother Superior used rude language with an Indian who was peddling fruit door to door. Elvin interceded on behalf of the Indian, but the nun then said that because they refused to fully accept the church, they were lower beings in the eyes of the lord, and must be treated firmly, like animals. Elvin told the nun that even animals deserve kindness and led Minerva straight to the barbershop, and had her hair cut like a boy's. He took Minerva on that expedition. She turned out to be a natural camper and became even better at dealing with the jungle than Elvin. She demanded to go on all subsequent expeditions. It was Minerva who made initial contact with the tribes, and many of the people that they met in the jungle would only really speak with her. She actually taught Elvin their dialects and manners."

Carl took over and passed the canteen to Mark.

"When we met in a class about the Yucatan, she told us that they had met the Yohimbe in the past and could closely predict when their next expedition off the reservation would take place. Neither of us knew she was Elvin's daughter for about a year. She introduced us to her father and he interviewed us in his famous lab. He told us that he had asked Minerva to invite us, telling her that she could bring her anthropologist friend, chase up a biologist, and that he knew a suitable a surgeon. He wanted to form a team to pose as students, while we are actually going to smuggle out the greatest medical discovery of all time!"

Mark spoke now, "Elvin has access to satellite images and the equipment to receive them on a special laptop, with which we used to find the tribe. We could see every campfire in the region at night with infra-red satellite images. Elvin supplied us with navigational devices and radios, and we would get out of the jungle in boats. He had it all planned out perfectly. We jumped at the opportunity to work with the Yohimbe! They are not afraid of the jungle, you know...not like I am."

Carl looked at Mark and said, "I think you are doing much better than I."

We listened to the people talking around us, and I was going to ask Carl about the victim of the operation, when we heard some kids shouting. We walked towards them to see that they were trying to catch a large scorpion. I was horrified at the sight, but Carl said, "Watch..."

One little boy with a stick the size of a well-used pencil managed to pin its tail. He then grabbed it by the body, with its stinger between his fingers. I was amazed at the boy's facility. Another child handed him a round piece of fruit, and he jabbed the scorpion's stinger into it and squeezed the poison out. Carl told me that this was how they collected one of the drugs that they used in the surgery.

"There are enzymes in the fruit that somehow combine with a part of the poison, and transform it into a kind of jelly that prepares the wound site during the operation."

The fruit was now discolored from the venom and another boy with a knife cut the bruised fruit away and put it into a metal can and sealed it with a piece of cut-rubber inner -tube, tied with cord. They had a can full of this stuff.

"Why do they let children handle scorpions?" I asked.

Mark said that either the Yohimbe are immune, or they have an antitoxin.

"Or they just dig, livin' on the edge! You should have seen them milking the huge fer-de-lance snakes into my old film cans."

Mark uncapped the lens on his camera. He took photos of the kids at work, and they told him their words for the fruit and the scorpion, which he repeated into a small cassette recorder.

I asked him how long they had been studying the tribe.

"We found them about two weeks ago, and I have been trying to learn everything about them as fast as I can."

I asked if it was a difficult language to learn, and he told me that he had studied the Mayan hieroglyphics and could read them, and

Minerva had taught him a lot, so he really only needed to get up to conversational speed.

"The weird part is that their written language is very grim stuff, all about death and the gods, but their spoken language seems to be ordered on humor, like every word can be changed to make it sound funny, or mean something funny, or rhyme in a funny way and they will try to make each other laugh, even when they are serious."

I told him that it sounded like the way the British act. He frowned and said, "Hmm"

I could not tell what that meant. We were chatting like that about their language when a group of women jogged into the area. They were crowding the area around the little old man sleeping in the hammock. An old woman and a younger one began tugging at his hair and shouting at him.

Mark was surprised. "That is the Chief, Eight Jaguar in that hammock... This is unprecedented. He never wakes up before four thirty or five." He was looking at his watch.

I stated that it did not look as if he had any choice.

"Well, his wives might not be able to do it anyway..."

I turned to see and he was right. It suddenly occurred to me that Eight Jaguar had probably slept through the helicopter delivery as well, and that had taken about fifteen minutes. I asked Mark if the old guy was dead, and now Carl was there too, with Minerva the botanist. Carl quickly introduced me to Minerva and she explained to us that the ladies had taken her to a place where they collect a type of flower for the operation when they were confronted by a giant cat, a jaguar, at least six feet long, with another three feet of tail. She made a ring with her hands to demonstrate the size of the paw print the cat left. Mark went over to the hut to listen to the old ladies as they rubbed something from a jar all over the Chief's nostrils and begin talking to him. Eight Jaguar was being forcibly awakened from what turned out to be a Blue Frog Trance, his favorite. We followed.

Mark listened and then turned to Minerva. "He did not charge you?"

Minerva turned her palms up and said, "That's the weird part, he just growled a few times and looked at us, the old ladies were terrified!"

We all looked at each other. Mark translated for Carl and I.

"The older wife is telling him that the leopard was eating the white smoke flowers." Minerva verified this and added that the flowers were a poisonous species. Now the witch doctor is describing a dream, one he has had many times, he is in the forest, no people are around. He is eating raw food."

Minerva broke off her translation and ran towards the women, speaking Yohimbe. I watched as Mark's lips slowly stopped moving, then the women began crying and shaking their heads.

Mark turned to Carl and I and said, "You'd better sit down. There has been a change of plans… Eight Jaguar feels that this huge cat in the forest is coming for him… He has decided that this giant cat will be the host body for his final Incarnation."

As I watched, I needed no translation when the Chief assembled a hunting expedition. The Chief called out names of his hunters and screeched encouragement to them. The hunters jogged in place and sang to the Chief. I lowered myself onto the dirt and watched as the old wives sobbed and pulled on Eight Jaguar's arms, and his hair as he explained his plan and the hunters turned and jogged off into the spongy forest.

Chapter 6: Eight Jaguar

People ask me all the time, "How do you surgeons get used to all the blood?" Well, it's like this: We don't. At least, not entirely. It's a question of context, really. The more common procedures are easier to do without being distracted by blood. The sight of blood can be terrifying if an artery is cut by mistake. It shoots out like a water pistol, in spurts timed with the heartbeat. I also become squeamish when I am apprehensive about my patient's chances of survival. But the idea of cutting into a wild animal disgusted me. I was terrified that it was going to be a gory, bloody mess. I was concerned enough already over issues like the possibility of infection, rejection of the graft, the appropriateness of the instruments I had available, even the availability of light, which could be threatened by clouds. Worse yet, I found myself worrying about those things that, in my disoriented state, I might forget. I pride myself in my excellent memory and it had never failed me, but I felt…naked… it's hard to describe.

In order to calm down his wives and the rest of us, the Chief called for a feast. I realized that it was dinnertime when the mats came out and baskets of food materialized from the trees. They skewered the fillets of large animals and they skewered small animals whole and planted the stakes around the pit. The Chief Eight Jaguar came out of his hammock and hobbled over to a fire ring. He took a smoldering stick out of the ashes and cupped his hand around the ember. He gave it a long steady puff, and it bore flames. He went before the pit, and threw his torch in. The flame slowly spread across the dome of logs, coating the kindling with a shimmering glow. The Chief watched the fire grow and then pulled a handful of something out of a bag and tossed it onto the logs. Then the fire began to pour up a vast quantity of thick light gray smoke, and a few women began to fan the fumes into the Chief's hut. The thick clouds drenched the venerable shaman, and I could just barely see him, gently waving his outstretched arms while taking long, laborious breaths, inhaling the smoke as deeply as he could. I realized that through the smoke, I could see Mark and some of the other men as well. Minerva and Carl were avoiding the scene like the plague.

I walked over to the botanist and asked her what the smoke was. She said "Tobacco" out the side of her mouth. I decided to go and try it. Mark was standing right next to the Chief. As I approached the crowd the smoke was just beginning to thin out, but I could just barely stand the smell, and my eyes watered profusely. I heard a giggle behind me and there was a Yohimbe man holding his breath with his eyes and cheeks bulging out. The other Indians were looking at me and they giggled too. A teen made "goggles" with his hands and held them up to his eyes, imitating my glasses. One little whelp was actually crying giant crocodile tears to mock me. I admit it was embarrassing. I asked Mark how he was doing and he said he was getting used to it, and that Carl had bad manners, and would not join us.

"Carl is running the risk of not seeming manly to them," Mark shared.

I asked Mark how often the Chief smokes. "Every day," he said.

Minerva later told me that the "Europeans" had introduced the stuff to the natives.

I pointed out that the "natives" introduced it to "us" as well.

She hesitated, and grinned at me. What a beautiful smile!

The smoke eventually cleared and the feast was under way. The Chief's attendants brought out a cape for him to wear, and it was fantastic. It was a metallic blue color and I saw that it was made of cloth covered with thousands of butterfly wings. Someone brought me a skewer with bits of meat on it. I was too hungry to wonder what it was, but it was delicious, mild tobacco flavor and all.

Carl sat with me and had a large leaf with three skewers on it. He told me that Mark had told the Indians to give him extra food because he was going to have a baby. Carl rolled his eyes when the kids brought even more, whispering and staring at his gut. A tiny girl put her ear on the side of Carl's belly and held her hand to her mouth to signal silence. We all became quiet. She turned to the other kids, and shook her head, and the kids all left.

"Help me with this," he said.

"What is it?" I asked.

Carl did not know exactly what the meat was but he said that they rolled the meat in honey before they cooked it. We drank water out of blue enameled tin cups that looked like antiques from the old west. I noticed that there were other trade goods around the campsite: machetes, cloth stitched together from faded rice sacks, steel pots, and I noticed that Atay was wearing a watch. He was talking with Mark, and then Mark turned and signaled for us to join them. We finished the tasty meal. Dogs ate the scraps, and the skewers went into the fire.

We went to a covered and partitioned area full of baskets. Each basket was full of tightly rolled scrolls. A small library. Atay began to take a few scrolls out of their baskets and unrolled one on the floor. It was completely covered with hieroglyphics. The details were so fine and complex that it was difficult to resolve individual characters. Mark and Atay began to read them, mumbling and pointing at the characters. Carl told me he was going to get the camera and I asked Mark what the hieroglyphics meant. He told me it was a genealogical chart, showing whom the donors had been for all the previous Incarnations, that apparently they all had to be from the same family. In a moment I was able to see the family branches in the maze of pictograms. The artists who created the document drew animals' heads, with little colored balls coming out of them. They represented the different Incarnations of the shamans. There was an Anaconda clan, and a Deer clan. I searched for the Jaguar line, and found it in an island, surrounded by other bloodlines. I asked Mark about it and he consulted with Atay.

As it turns out, he told us, the family of the host bodies for Eight Jaguar has mixed blood with "the civilized people," and are thus unfit donors. I inferred that this was why the doctor was willing to be reincarnated into the body of an animal. Or why he was willing to let us participate. Then Atay opened a scroll depicting the operation itself. The scroll was life size and showed extraordinary detail. It took a moment for me to make sense of the image that I saw, but I began to pick out details that I could recognize. The saw-tooth incision was clear, and the nerve branches coming out of the spine were anatomically accurate and precise. There were details of the most delicate tissues, and I was astounded to see that they had somehow managed to depict the invisible details of the individual neuron material itself. There was a stylized drawing of a nerve axon with hungry looking synapses around it, each one receiving a neurotransmitter.

I wondered how the artists could represent these tiny things without a microscope. Perhaps they had seen a modern medical textbook. I still wonder. At each synaptic gap was a series of leaves, or a spider, or a snake. Mark was telling me details of the notes that surrounded the body in the picture, but I wasn't really listening, just nodding and staring. We spent hours studying and discussing the scrolls. It had gotten dark. Mark had been taking pictures of each scroll the whole time, but gradually the darkness outside grew so that the camera's flash lit up the area.

A crowd of natives gathered to watch the flashes. Minerva gave a short speech to them explaining the flash, and taught the crowd to say "Oooh" and "Ahhh" in time with the flashes.

The strangely familiar and almost musical response to the camera shutter made Carl and me laugh, and seemed to make Mark's job more difficult. He had a hard time taking each photograph when a crowd was eagerly anticipating the next flash. He looked from side to side before taking the shot. Soon a few more people filed into the hut. I almost fell over when I realized that the newcomers were all tattooed with the scars of the Incarnación!

I said, "These new guys all have the scar!" under my breath, to Mark and Carl.

Mark looked up from the camera, "Oh, yeah. They got here yesterday, but left this morning to go to a temple near here to pray."

Atay was apparently going to lead the operation, Mark said, and the assistants watched as Atay pointed to various parts of the scroll and described the process to the others. He was sort of coaching his group of apprentice surgeons, and the guests, for they had to work quickly and simultaneously in order to bring the whole thing off. I was fascinated to see that the operation basically consisted of incisions made at very specific points along the spine, where very dense cartilage would make the cutting very difficult. I asked Carl if we should get Minerva. Mark heard the question and told me that they would not allow the women to read or even see the manuscripts.

"It has something to do with the fact that women can have babies and men can't"

I said "Oh, " even though the answer did not entirely satisfy me.

Along the sides of the body in the picture was another series of little flowers and leaves, and these were the applications of the various plant extracts used in the operation. Next to some of the flowers were scorpions, frogs or snakes, representing the venom used as well. There were a total of twenty-two scrolls. Some were all about the plants, one scroll showed the pit the Indians had prepared, some were about animals and some were just writing. After the "anatomical" scroll, the one with the microscopic detail, the other really fascinating one was a giant calendar. It was drawn on two scrolls, which were aligned to show a circular calendar, about two yards across. It showed hundreds of animals and abstract forms in different segments of the chart, and at one of the white lines that divided the circle into thirds, there was an empty gap. This gap, said Atay, marks tomorrow, the day of the operation. It is an 'empty day' that we can use to switch souls.

The assistants and Atay discussed the operation and at one point someone had to lie down across the floor so that Atay and the other Incarnated ones could show the others how to feel their way along his back, finding the rib sockets where the cuts would be made. They never did produce a chart showing how the operation could be performed on an animal like the jaguar that the women had described, but I knew that all mammals are similar in body structure, and apparently so did they. The Chief himself never did show up. He simply ate and ate, supposedly in preparation for the operation. It was late when I stepped outside to get some air. The fire had died down and the Shaman was sitting in his hut surrounded by women and some of the other Incarnated ones. Minerva was there, dressed in a robe like the other women wore. She had flowers in her hair and I looked at her for a long time. The women had shaved the Chief's head. The Chief saw me and called out to me.

"Doctor Germain!"

I was startled to hear the sound of his voice, so nasal and high, imitate a deep Gringo accent so well. It was Elvin William's voice. He was motioning for me to come over, laughing at my disoriented reaction to his trick. I almost slipped on some mud and all of the ladies giggled. One of them started whispering to the group in general.

Minerva told me that the Chief would grant an audience, and that I had better mind my manners. Her voice was cool and serious. I was going to ask her what good manners are to the Yohimbe, but Eight Jaguar began talking, in his own voice. Minerva translated.

"You came to see the Incarnation, so that you can help Mr. Williams… now we must ask you, has he exorcised the body of the donor yet?"

I was shocked that he had brought up so casually a subject that had troubled me so much, and I was unable to answer the question. Minerva spoke with the Chief briefly, then she told me not to worry about it. I looked at her, and she listened to the Chief. She asked me if I am honest. I said "Um…yes? "

Eight Jaguar said "mmm" and shut his eyes tightly, making fun of me. Minerva started giggling and I turned away, almost blushing. Eight Jaguar quickly shouted a question at Minerva and she turned and asked me if I found her attractive. I stared at Minerva, sort of embarrassed.

"I…find you..?"

"You're being rude," she said, "no pressure."

I looked at the Chief and his wives and the gaze of the other Incarnated ones, and I said, "Tell the Shaman that I want to make a baby with you!"

This was not the way I normally talked, and I surprised myself when I said it. Minerva was genuinely shocked, but she laughed and said, "Alright!" and she told the Chief.

The wives and their husband all said, "Heee, " which is how the Yohimbe brag. One of the other witch doctors then asked if I had been in a trance recently.

I said, "No, " and Eight Jaguar told the youngest of his wives to go and get him something. She returned with an old beat up canteen and he untied a patch of inner tube rubber that the bottle was sealed with. He asked me to lean over, close to him. I thought he was going to whisper something, but I felt him tug on my hair. I pulled away instinctively and noticed that he was stuffing a lock of my hair into the canteen. I felt the side of my head and was aghast at the nearly bald spot on my head. My hair is not long and I certainly could not afford to lose a chunk of it. He had produced a knife out of thin air— at least I never saw it—and took my hair in a fraction of a second. He covered the mouth of the jar with his hand and shook it. His palm was wet with water as he took it off the jar. He held his palm out and he looked at it. The hut was silent. We all looked at the drops of iridescent water in Eight Jaguar's hand. When I leaned closer to see the sparkling drops of water, he quickly raised his hand under my face, and slapped my forehead, really hard. I fell back onto my butt and heard all the Yohimbe ladies talking and Minerva laughing, and as I tried to get up, Minerva said, "Rub your head! The doctor is telling you to rub your head! "

So I sat there rubbing the wet spot on my head, a point above and between my eyebrows, in a clockwise direction. I stared at the old bald Chief. He had a halo of tiny spots around his skull, where his ancient brain had been inserted into what had once been a fine young body. I watched his mouth move, and I felt like I could understand him, even though I did not know the meanings of the individual words. I didn't notice it for a long time, but I could not hear a single word anyone was saying. I became terrified, but I could not remember how to move my mouth. It felt as if my skin was smooth from my nose to my jaw, as if I had no mouth. I watched Mark bring Minerva a blanket. She put it on me, and then I could hear her saying that I was falling asleep. I leaned back onto the mats and the last thing I saw was Eight Jaguar, smiling at me, clapping his hands with my heartbeat as it slowed down. He and his wives were singing to me and the tempo slowed down again, and as I fell asleep, I was terrified that the Chief would clap his hands even slower and then stop, causing my heart to go quiet. The clapping stopped. My eyes opened and there was a ring of children around me. Everyone was gone and the jungle was full of fog. It was dawn.

One of the children was white and I realized that it was me, as a little boy. He had torn clothes and shaggy hair, and as I watched, he held the hair up off his forehead, revealing an open hole in his skull, in the same spot where the Shaman had slapped me. I stared at the opening and could see his gray brain. There was no trace of blood.

The young me, about in fifth grade, spoke, "The doctor is coming... do you know what to do?"

Then a huge leopard leaped out of the jungle and crushed me to the ground. As I fought the giant cat, I saw the boys all watching, but not doing anything. The jaguar's mouth was just over my head and when I closed my eyes I felt its teeth pierce the spot that had been slapped. My ears were filled with its roar. Now the Eighth Incarnación of the Jaguar Chief stood before me. He wore the golden gown that Elvin had described to me. He took me by the hand and led me to the operation pit. The scene turned out to be exactly as it was to be the next day, I later realized. The cat was barely visible in the pit and the wound was near the surface. Dappled sunlight hovered around us; the sun was not directly overhead yet. I saw the Chief, face down, next to the pit. We were cutting his spine away and as one person cut, a wife of the Chief dripped a solution from a jar onto the tissue. The Eighth Jaguar stood next to me and told me to look closer, and as I looked, I realized that I could see the details of the incision with perfect clarity, as if I was looking through some kind of binoculars. The tiny obsidian blades the natives used made perfect cuts, and I could see the tissues, the cells and then, magically, even the molecules of the cells themselves.

I saw the potions and extracts breaking open the chains of molecules, and I saw the damaged matter of cells ruptured by the blades floating away, leaving a fresh living surface of healthy cells exposed. I saw how each potion had a role in fusing the cells of the implant spine into the new host body. The water in the pit was a plasma of oxygen, enzymes, hormones and sugars created by the millions of tiny chemical factories within the flowers and spiders of the jungle. I was able to see the molecular bonds of the individual cell walls forming, as if by magic. The undamaged nerves were left with their synapses reaching out into empty space itself. When the cells of the Chief's spine aligned with the cells of the cat's body, the synapses met and the organs began to function as one unit, with nerve impulses flowing along the seamless chain of neuron matter almost instantly, as if it had never been broken. In school I had learned how to mend tissues on the scale of the scalpel, then the scale of the microscope, and had felt pride in the acquisition of my knowledge, but now I was witnessing the art of surgery at an infinitely smaller scale. I felt like Dante being led through the nether realms, by my guide, the Shaman.

Then we rose out of the scene and I could see the huge jaguar, being operated on. Then the scene grew dark.

I was now falling through space itself. I was in a perfectly black realm where I could not see my hands before me. I was marveling at the silence when I realized that there was a humming sound around me. A deep throbbing drone. I turned my head to locate it, but it was everywhere, and slowly getting louder. Then I realized that there was a dim light before me, way off in the distance. I felt myself floating and not falling any longer, and I relaxed. The dim light before me grew brighter, and the sound grew louder. The light before me looked like a long thin object. It was slowly twisting and I could see that it was a long ropelike strand of small yellow lights. As I watched, the object floated towards me and grew to fill my entire field of vision. I saw that the millions of lights were arranged in a series of curving rows that wrapped around each other, and the thundering sound washed through me and made my whole body shake. The brightness of the lights around me became so intense that I tried to shield my eyes. And then the thing began to crush me. I felt that I would be flattened, but then I slipped through a gap between some of the glowing elements, and I saw that there was a lot of space between each light. The entire object was made of the small flickering lights of slightly differing shades of color, with great areas of darkness between them. The object was a molecule. I love chemistry, and I could easily recognize the patterns and designs and remember them from a representation of a DNA molecule, deoxyribonucleic acid. I was inside an immense model of the most important element of life itself. The very first living thing, the first object on our planet that could reproduce itself. The lights were twinkling all around me in a huge tunnel-shaped space that filled my entire horizon, and I realized that most of the molecule was composed of empty space.

Energy itself held the whole apparatus together, and I could see that we are all composed of nothing more than tiny traces of energy, and vast amounts of absolutely empty space. And every atom in the molecule is mostly composed of empty space as well. We are mostly nothing. Nothing at all but emptiness itself. The very fact that we exist is based on a foundation of nothingness. We are each of us a castle in the clouds, a castle of clouds, with a mad king in the throne hall, lording over an illusion, thinking it is an empire. I became sad, and a feeling of intense remorse and regret washed over me very quickly. I became nauseated. I wanted to cry or curl up into a ball and hold onto my knees like a fetus, but I was incapacitated by the fascinating sight and the waves of sound that became quieter and quieter, and the ocean of small lights began to fade away. I was not afraid anymore. I watched the massive DNA molecule float away and I began to feel better, and could regain the illusion that I am made of a solid substance and that I am a real object in the universe. This is the first time I have ever told this part of the dream to anyone.

The scene suddenly changed, and my sense of being alone and lost left me entirely. I thought I was awake. Thank God! Eight Jaguar asked me if I understood, and I said yes, but that I was afraid. He suddenly transformed himself into Doctor Arthur Cook, my dear dead friend. I became emotional at the very sight of him. He did not stop smiling at me, but I heard his voice within my mind, "You'll know just what to do when you are there." This was just the sort of thing he would have said. I felt like crying, and I closed my eyes.

When I opened them, it was Eight Jaguar before me again, staring at me with his funny eyes bulging out, and crying like a cheap soap opera star. I felt stupid and angry. Then he turned into a small boy and looked at me casually, and cut a fart. Then he ran into the forest and disappeared, chattering like a monkey. My feelings were bruised at his callous act, but I couldn't help laughing at the prank. I laughed harder and harder. I was laughing through tears of pain. The chattering grew louder and louder and I woke up, with children pulling on my hair and shouting "Doctor Germain! Doctor Germain!" in their tiny voices. I was still laughing, and the kids were wiping my eyes, and one was looking into my eyes, and he was crying too.

The sun was up and there was a lot going on. I was still thinking about my dreams when Mark appeared. "So the doctor has your spirit in his jar now... how does it feel?" Mark looked like a wired coffee addict, was talking quickly. He looked like he had been crying too. I could not answer right away. Then I said,

"My spirit?"

"That's right, my friend. Do you know how the operation works now?"

"I think so..."

"Well you'd better, because you're the only one he told." He bugged his eyes out and nodded.

I thought for a moment and asked, "What about Atay?"

Then Mark looked down and told me that Atay was dead.

I shouted, "What?" and actually gagged on some water I was drinking.

"The giant cat came last night and killed him. There was a terrible fight, and the Chief shot the cat with a poisoned dart."

Mark told me to hold my hands over my head to help me breathe, and he said, "The hunters had been chasing the animal all night long, and when they realized that the cat had led them on a giant goose chase all the way back here to the camp, they realized that the cat was going to attack the village, and they did not know who the beast was going for. They whistled ahead as loud as they could to alert the village and the only person who heard it was the Chief, who was awake... you slept through it."

"What about the other Incarnated people?" I asked.

"They are gone. They felt that the death of Atay was a bad omen."

Mark and Atay had apparently been buddies and it was painful to see him so sad. I asked Mark how he knew that Eight Jaguar had "told me" about the operation.

He said that Eight Jaguar had bragged that he would do it, after he had dosed me with his "Dream Water."

Carl helped me stand up and we went to see the pit. The leopard was sleeping in it and his tail was slowly twitching, making the water swirl. The jaguar's back and head had already been shaved, and I had the distinct feeling that I had missed a lot of the preparation. Some of the men had dragged the Chief next to the pit. Mark told me that Eight Jaguar had anesthetized himself with a dart. The fire had changed the color of the clay and the bottom of the pit was full of water. The leopard's nostrils had been plugged with large seeds and a section of old garden hose was coming out of its mouth at an angle which suggested that it had been intubated to maintain an airway. Two of the wives sat near his head. One sang and the other blew into the hose regularly. Bubbles floated to the surface around the cat's head as she blew air into its chest. The women had painted their faces white, except for rings around their eyes, and they looked like skeletons. I realized that they were already treating the cat as if it was their husband.

Minerva was talking to Carl about the death of Atay as they walked over to me.

"I did not know it would be like this," Minerva said.

I told her that I had no idea what to expect any more. I was rubbing my stomach. I was physically hungry, but the idea of food made me ill. Minerva was looking at me.

"Do you think you can ... do it?"

I looked at her and before I could think of an answer, I said, "Sure! Do you think I'm stupid?"

Carl and Minerva turned to each other. Mark raised his eyebrows at me.

I rethought my answer and started to tell them about my dream. "Look, last night, in my dream, Eight Jaguar showed me how the chemicals work. It's all based on the maintenance of living tissue with an artificial plasma, and removal of damaged tissues to prevent infection and set a perfect graft. Most of these solutions simply act like blood itself, to keep the undamaged cell matter alive during the operation.

"In my dream, the ladies were scooping the fluid up in jars and shaking it to keep it oxygenated, they would pour it back along the wound site. One solution, the one with scorpion venom to be exact, is used to strip damaged cell matter away from the site of the incisions. After the host body and donor nervous system are joined, the remaining healthy cells of each can then mate up without the obstacle of damaged cell matter in the way. Healing is accelerated by the fact that the dead and damaged tissue is already gone. All that's left to do is heat the subject and that's it; the cutting is the easy part; it's the chemicals that do the tricky part."

The biologist, the botanist and the anthropologist looked at each other. Carl then asked, as if for clarity, "Then you're saying that these liquids are like microscopic scalpels and sutures?"

"Exactly," I replied.

Chapter 7: The Incarnación

Well, we got off to a rocky start. Apparently all the Indians had the impression that I was supposed to know everything. When the other shamen had arrived the night before, I had felt so relieved, I hoped that they would do the work, and I could learn from them. When they disappeared, I felt a crushing sense of desperation, but I was able to calm myself down and not frighten the rest of the team. Somehow the rumor among the Yohimbe was that I was the last person the shaman visited, and thus had information critical to the operation. They had assumed it would be Atay. They had practiced with him, I guessed. To re-orient myself with the specifics of the juices I was to be using, I got the scrolls out and had Mark and one of the Yohimbe translate. Mark brought over one of the young boys who had been watching from the shadows the night before.

"This is Po-Asu, the apprentice to Atay. He has memorized all the plants and can read the scrolls, but he is really nervous."

I looked at Po-Asu and I asked him why he was afraid, and Mark answered that the boy was afraid of what would happen to him after the Incarnation, that the jaguar might come for him. I reminded him that after the operation, the beast would have their Chiefs' brain and he would remember Po-Asu well and not eat him.

I asked them where the yellow flower potion was, because we needed it first. Mark translated that the men did not know.

I asked the boy if we could let Minerva see the scrolls, now that Atay was gone. After some long discussion about it with Mark, Po-Asu admitted that Eight Jaguar would have allowed it.

"All the women liked Atay…" he reasoned.

The anthropologist went to get her and came back with Carl too, who seemed to be trying not to laugh, and I could see that the botanist did not look too thrilled. She asked the Young boy why he wanted to have a lock of her hair. Po-Asu bragged that he had strong magic and will make her love him, and that this is his price for letting a woman see the scrolls. Mark was translating and we looked at each other. Po-Asu's friends were giggling, but he tuned them out. He was twelve years old, and looked very serious, for a Yohimbe. It was imperative that Minerva accept the deal because we needed her to see the scrolls. We knew where to use the extracts, but only the women knew which potions were in which pots. Or even where all the pots were. The women, Eight Jaguars' wives, had always participated eagerly in surgery, one of the men said, "The ladies used to get a fresh young husband, but now they are losing their man—to the jungle! We needed their help, we would have accepted anything to do his bidding."

As Po-Asu and Minerva discussed the deal, I realized that our botanist was driving a hard bargain. The boy began to stammer and shake his head. He lost his cool demeanor as he considered what Minerva was saying, and when he seemed to be vulnerable, Minerva took off her hat. She had short spikey, copper red hair. Po-Asu stared at it. We all did. Then he said, "O.K." Minerva took a Swiss army knife out of her pocket, folded out a pair of scissors, and asked me to take a snip at the back, "Where it won't show. "

I stood there like a dope for a moment and Mark finally whispered, "Go for it, dude!"

Carl squeaked.

Minerva said, "Well?"

I cut a snip and handed it to Po-Asu. He took off his necklace and tied the lock to it. Minerva left and came back with all of Eight Jaguar's wives. I figured that maybe Po-Asu would have a lot of explaining to do, but when he showed off his necklace, the other men might understand.

I asked Mark if he thought we were interfering with their cultural system, and Mark responded in a deep voice, "Dammit Jim, I'm a doctor, not a philosopher."

I smiled and said, "Sure, Bones."

The women seemed somewhat mystified by the scrolls, but Minerva was able to make some sense of them, the way Mark had. They found the calendar scrolls, fitted them together, and were apparently on familiar ground. They began to sing a song about all of the months and seasons, naming the dozens of little faces as they went. They found one that I had not noticed from the night before. It was apparently a special one because the men tried to keep it hidden, but the ladies had it unrolled and after a moment of puzzled searching, Minerva announced that this one was some sort of map of what is inside a woman! She pointed to some mythical looking animal inside the cartoon woman's belly, and told the ladies that it was a frog whose throat could puff up, and this was why women puffed up when they were pregnant. The old ladies looked at the men and shook their heads, smiling and muttering to each other. I could tell that we had opened a real can of worms and then I saw Po-Asu looking up. The sun was climbing and the light was near the pit. I went to him and we looked at the Chief, sleeping on the mats, and the giant cat in the pit next to him. The Yohimbe began to gather around the pit and they seemed to know it was time.

The ladies began to bring pots, bottles, canteens, an old gas can and many gourds out of their huts and out of the bushes. Minerva and I looked at each other across the pit and realized that we were performing this operation together, and we seemed to be alright with that. She asked me what we needed first. I named a potion, and she conferred with the women. They produced a coffee can full of what looked like grease, and smelled like urine. Po-Asu and two other boys and an old man took some of it and painted it onto the back of the jaguar, in the area around its spine. As they worked, the cat bobbed in the water and one of them had to hold the animal steady. The cat had pale gray skin under its black fur. Minerva and I took some of the potion and began to apply it to the Chief.

I asked Carl to get my bag. As if on cue, one of the men brought me a roll of cloth and untied it. Inside were about twenty tiny scalpels. They had obsidian blades and bone handles. They were tied with coarse thread and were translucent near the edge. There were some wooden wedges of different widths. Mark placed my bag next to me and some of my equipment was passed around the group and examined. I had brought spreaders, clamps, suction bulbs, cannula, sponges, suturing material, and lots of other accessories. I was slightly uneasy about how to proceed, but because of the tour the Chief had given me in my dream, I felt as if the operation was an indelible part of my memory. I told the women to add the yellow flower potion to the water around the jaguar. This signified the start of the operation. They poured it out of a thermos bottle. I asked them to put hot rocks into the water and we began cutting away the skin around the spines of both bodies. The women wanted to work on the Chief. I decided to work on the cat, figuring that I would learn a little bit about feline anatomy as we exposed the bones.

The Yohimbe apparently had plenty of practice. They worked silently and quickly. The skin of the old man was cut away in a wide area around the spine but the incision down the cat's back was zigzagged tightly around the spinal branches. The Yohimbe had not needed me to tell them what the saw was for. They used it to cut the top off of the skull of the cat. The women got to work on the Chief. They began at the coccyx, cutting it away from the hipbone and working their way up, as men went the other way down the spine of the cat. The tiny blades of the curved scalpels the Yohimbe used were fantastically suited to the task and the surgeons could slide them under the spine to cut it free with a stroke by gently prying it between the joints and cutting up through the cartilage. The design caused the blade to follow the path of least resistance. They used each scalpel a few times.

I discarded my straight steel scalpel and a Yohimbe taught me the technique. A fast pace is the key to the Incarnation. In conventional medicine, we put the patient under anesthesia and proceed at a stately pace, suctioning blood as we go, pausing for refreshments, making sure we don't close up the patient with a retractor still in there. The Yohimbe don't mind if a drop of sweat falls on the patient, which was inevitable as the water heated up and the sun stood over us. As soon as the cat's spine was free, we rolled the beast over in the water and its entire nervous system was dislodged, into the brown-red solution. The spine was pulled to the side and the cat's optic nerves were cut at the brain and left dangling, as were the lesser nerve tissues. The cat's spine and brain were then pulled out of the pit and taken away in a banana leaf, by an old man. The cat was then pushed to the bottom of the pit and the Chief, with his brain exposed and spine cut free was lowered into the pit, literally on top of the cat. We gently rolled him over, then dislodged the human's brain and spine as we had done with the cat. As if in a movie, I saw the Chief's corpse being hauled out of the pit by old men. At this point I knew that my dream with Eight Jaguar was taking over.

Two of the women had taken up the optic nerves of the jaguar and the optic nerves of the shaman's floating central nervous system. They used a reed to hold the nerves as they cut a long incision down their length. The slitted nerve strands were painted with green liquid and wound together. While the optic nerves were being grafted, I trimmed some material off the top and sides of the Chief's brain, so it would fit in the smaller cavity of the cat's skull.

I knew that what I was cutting away was the Chief's very humanity. Once the brain was fitted, in what was perhaps the most disgusting moment of my entire life, red potion was painted around the skullcap and it was replaced. The wooden wedges that the Yohimbe use are to force the ribs of the host body to fit the donor spine. I began to measure the distances between the jaguar's ribs with my finger and had Po-Asu trim the wedges. I cut slices into the muscle between the ribs, and inserted the wedges. When the rib sockets in the Chief's spine were aligned with the jaguar's ribs, we coated the joint with the black potion, and tied string around the bones to hold the joint together. The wood was a relative of balsa and had been soaked in "Termite Potion" which cause it to dissolve within a week. The string used to tie the spine together was similar. I saw that the tailbone of the human spine

JOHN GAMBOA

would have to be joined to the tail of the cat. We removed the tip of the coccyx and exposed the spinal cord. I bathed it with "Red Potion" and "Banana Flower Extract," and swabbed the cavity at the cat's tail with the same.

We pressed the last of the spine in place and folded the skin over the site.

A young girl brought us a branch of a tree swarming with huge ants. There was honey on the stick and the ants were stuck to it, waving their free arms. The Yohimbe began picking off the ants and holding their giant mandibles up to the incision, which they pressed together. As soon as the ant bit down, the surgeon would pinch its thorax and abdomen off. The ant's head remained, biting the wound shut. The best thing about these sutures is that they could be placed extremely quickly and working together, we had the entire site closed, with over ten sutures an inch, in about five minutes. When the work was done the women began bailing out the old water near the animal's tail and pouring in fresh water near the cat's head. Fresh potions were mixed into the water, and as the new solution replaced the old, new hot rocks were added and the shakers resumed their work of aerating the fluid and pouring it over the wound. I looked at Minerva, she was wiping off her arms with a towel, and we smiled at each other for the first time. Carl clocked the whole event, from the first incision to the last suture, at twenty-seven minutes.

The Yohimbe got up and began to replace the bloody mats around the pit.

Minerva and I got up and watched as they began to clean up the area. They were planning on leaving soon and I wondered if they were going to rehabilitate the monster we had created, or just abandon it. I felt a rush of inordinately strong anxiety wash over me at the thought of this. I saw that the women kept blowing air into the giant cats' lungs and they kept singing their sweet bird songs to him. I looked at the mat I was sitting on and ran my hand over it. It was as smooth as vinyl. As I looked at it I realized that to me it symbolized the sophistication that the Yohimbe possessed that I had not expected

72

to find when I first got there. I felt that it would be normal to cry. A fair hand covered my fingers. Minerva was pulling me back to my feet. I stood up and said "What?"

"Everyone is going to the funeral for Eight Jaguar." I followed, but Minerva did not let go of my hand. We seemed to be walking straight into the dense undergrowth of the jungle, but there was a path patted into the foliage by the passage of many feet.

Minerva spoke softly as we picked our way through the matted leaves and roots. "The Yohimbe have decided that they need to cremate the Chief's corpse, so the Jaguar cannot eat him."

We arrived at a very small clearing and saw that a group of Yohimbe had been hard at work, probably all night. There was a huge pyre of hardwood, and the Chief's body was on top of it.

Mark was taking photographs, but he looked up when Minerva and I got there. I think the group had been waiting for us. One of the Chief's widows produced a yellow disposable lighter and snapped it and lit the base of the woodpile. As the smoke rose and the flames crackled, I could smell tobacco. Within a minute, the thick milky smoke was drenching us and many of the Yohimbe were crying, and Carl, Mark, Minerva and I were crying too.

As the flames of the funeral pyre grew hotter and hotter, the crowd receded into the woods. I have no idea how the people accomplished this because the vegetation was so thick, but Minerva led me along a smooth path that I did not recognize. Minerva was silent, and I could hear the Yohimbe in the distance, singing to the Jaguar in the pit. Suddenly I saw bright light ahead where the trees seemed to end and we arrived at the river. The other bank was about a hundred yards away, and the water moved slowly in the middle. The blue gray clay of the pit was here, and the water was gently sloshing the banks as the sunlight made wavy patterns on the bottom. I turned to speak with her. She was nude. I stared at her and she looked at me as if it were a joke.

I had gotten a good look at her face when I first met her, and I thought she was pretty - and I had joked about making babies with her to impress the Yohimbe, but I had not really taken the opportunity to ogle or fantasize about her. I had been sort of busy.

73

"How can you stand having that slimy crap all over you?" She asked. She walked into the river and I stared at her. I actually looked around before I undressed. Minerva was up to her belly in the water and I waded toward her. The current was very gentle and the water was warm and had a silky feeling to it. As we got further out she began to swim but I walked along the bottom, feeling the clay under my toes, and the river pushing at me. She began swimming upstream and I followed. As she swam, her butt surfaced in the tan water. She turned and we grinned at each other. A little way up the bank from where our clothes were, a flat rock rose out of the water. As we approached it, a giant iguana climbed off and plopped into the water and swam dogpaddle style and watched us as he drifted by. Minerva stepped out of the water and walked up onto the rock. She petted the water out of her hair and sat down on the warm stone. I knelt next to her, and she pulled me to her. She kissed me as we looked into each other's eyes. I shut my eyes as I lay back on the smooth boulder next to her and she began to climb onto me. I could see the bright blue sky above us as we made love and as she moved, her shadow blocked the sun. I felt my fear of the jungle melt away.

Minerva was at home in the forest and as her body was pressing against mine, I could feel the things that had terrified me, the noises, the insects, the shadows, all revealing themselves as nurturing, abundant and magical in her presence. For a moment I think I fell asleep, with her body on mine. When I opened my eyes, Minerva was looking at me, petting my hair back away from my eyes. And in the fraction of a second it took me to see it, I saw love in her eyes. She had the most beautiful smile I'd ever seen, and I became self-conscious and apprehensive.

Then that look I had seen, one of serenity and joy, was gone and I realized that I had failed to seize the moment and return her simple happiness. I realize now that it was only because the experience of joy was foreign to me, and I did not recognize it. But in that moment, I was pathetic. Here was a woman who had offered herself to me and given me a gift so sweet, and for some reason, I did not accept it. Then she looked at me as if she had just asked me to add two and two and was waiting for an answer. I sat up next to her and looked at her breasts, her throat, her face and I stammered:

"Are we... I mean... do you have a... um..."

"What? A condom?" She had obviously developed her sense of humor around the Yohimbe. She continued, "It's too late for that." She looked around and there was a silence between us. I could hear the faint lapping of the river. She looked right into my eyes and told me that I was most likely a great student but that I had obviously never learned anything about girls. I opened my mouth. I heard myself asking her just what our 'relationship' was. I don't remember how I was asking her this, but she interrupted me.

"We are guests of the Yohimbe in the rainforest, so we are bound by Yohimbe custom. I declared for you yesterday and was actually challenged by some of the young women. They wanted you because you are very brave and they think you are funny looking and the people tell jokes about you and imitate the way you walk around watching where your feet go. Now you are mine and the other ladies had better leave you alone. When we leave the rainforest I guess you can do as you wish but I think you and I should continue to be an item."

And that was it. She was totally nonchalant, and I found that even more confusing.

"You mean we are like...Married?"

Minerva nodded her head.

"Because we had sex?"

She nodded again, "Because now you could be my baby's father."

I was stunned by this statement, and I felt as if I had been manipulated. I was trying to figure out a way to put this into words, but Minerva was way ahead of me.

"Doctor Germaine did you know that all mammals achieve fertilization via sexual conjunction?"

I said, "Huh? I mean, of course I know th   ..."

"And, Doctor Germaine, did you or did you not, of your own free will, engage in sexual union, with me about ten minutes ago?" I nodded, smiling and looked at the water flowing by.

She used the voice of an English gentleman and said, "Then take responsibility, son. Do the right thing!"

She stood up and I gazed at her belly, as if I was trying to see if there was already a baby Victor or Victoria in there. Then she turned and stepped into the water. I followed her, not talking. When we got to the riverbank where our clothes were, she held my elbow and petted the water off my skin. I felt her hands sweeping the drops down my arms, down my back. I began to pet the water off her too.

No one noticed when we got back to the camp. I went to the pit where the giant cat with a human brain lay. I was not nauseated any more and felt much more optimistic about the experiment. The women had been adding hot rocks because the animal wasn't breathing well. I went to my bag and got my stethoscope and discovered that it works underwater. Some of the fluid had gotten into the cat's lungs. We slid our arms under the cat and inclined it to drain the fluid. I put one hand under the cat and pressed on his chest with the other one. The cat belched out some water and I heard his breathing return to normal. I removed the tube in his throat and had the women support the muzzle of the cat so he could breathe unassisted. Looking back, I realized that our problem was that our pit was dug for a human who would be laying face down, but the cat was lying on its side because its legs were in the way when they were under it.

I decided to examine my patient. The thousands of tiny ant heads that held the incision shut looked like a zipper going down the animal's back. I looked very closely. In normal circumstances, the skin would be inflamed and discolored and there would be tiny opened capillaries, which can be slow to heal, because they deliver the fewest clotting agents to the site. But this skin was smooth, of uniform color, and very healthy looking. The other thing I noticed was that the hair we had shaved was growing back at an accelerated rate. I poured water over the scalp and did not see any fresh blood. This impressed me very much because all scalp wounds bleed post-op, due to the volume and pressure of the blood in the cranial zone. I found myself beginning to have faith in this operation. I felt the dormant presence of Dr. Germaine reawakening within me, and I decided to give the beast point 3 cubic centiliters of Epinephrine, subcutaneous. As I worked, I realized that the women were watching what I was doing.

I took another 10-cc syringe from my bag and tore its package open. I showed them how the tip went on and the plunger could come out, then I took off the sharp, reinserted the plunger and I sucked some of the fluid from the pit into the barrel and squirted them with it. I gave it to them. They giggled. I think they really liked the syringe. Later on, the women of the tribe took all of the syringes that I had in the box, and then they began ransacking all my other medical equipment bags, removing the scissors, suture sets, scalpels, swabs, hemostats, ENT scope and flashlight, the gauze, the gloves, which some of them wore, they took the meds, and I wondered if I should try to explain them. I never did.

All I got back was my Holmes and Sutton Royal Attaché Case, containing nothing but some twigs and pebbles that were collected by children. I completed the injection and the women rubbed gently on the wart it left. I passed around the Epinephrine and they shook it, looked through it and passed it back, unimpressed. We were silent for a moment and it got awkward, then a young lady began to look at me and sing me the songs and chants that they had been singing to the Chief. Their music was silly and they did not sound very enthusiastic, and they did not seem to be able to agree on the tone or the rhythm, and the sound was almost irritating, but it was also pathetic and sad, and I decided that it was probably more difficult to sing off-key and out of syncopation than in harmony. I decided to join in. Minerva brought me food. She sat on the mat next to me and listened to us sing. After a while the yelping died down, we all began to eat and she of the lily white and gently freckled hands asked me if I wanted to know what the songs meant.

I said, "Yes, please."

"Right before you got here, the Chief made up the first part of the song and it goes, 'Wake up! Wake up! Come back to us and catch butterflies and smoke tobacco!' And the second part is total gibberish, but the old fart insisted that his wives sing it to him, exactly as he sang it."

I had been able to tell the difference when the ladies sang the gibberish parts and I asked Minerva if he had composed the last part after killing the leopard. This part of the song was very high - pitched and melodious and when I tried to sing it my voice had sounded like a loud whisper. She thought for a moment, asked the ladies to confirm her hunch, and said yes.

"Then perhaps it's cat talk."

Minerva was stunned by this idea and she told the ladies, who covered their mouths and squealed. That night Minerva brought me to her tent. She could tell that I was nervous and saw me looking at the Yohimbe women as she led me to bed. The old ladies were staring at us and chattering, but Minerva calmed me down by telling me that the natives had sent kids to spy on us in the river, so everyone knew.

"Everyone?" I asked, feeling victimized, "By tomorrow, everyone," Minerva said, as she was zipping the door shut.

The next morning, I awoke to the sound of the ladies singing to their Chief. I opened my eyes and stared at the roof of the tent, at Minerva. We got dressed and went outside. I was not prepared for the experience of waking up in the jungle... It was almost silent. No squeaking, buzzing insect noises, or squawking bird noises, or monkey howls, no shadows, it was velvety quiet and the fog was still nestled in the denser areas all around us. A jungle in the morning is not quite awake yet. There is a night crowd, and there is a day crowd, but the dawn was only there for the Yohimbe, I guessed. And it was really peaceful. I went to the pit and was smiling at the ladies and listening to their singing and looking at the cat when I realized that the beast's tail was moving.

Only the last foot of it. I fell to my knees, then to my chest, near the edge of the pit. I plunged my arms into the solution and pulled the cat's tail towards me. I brought it up to my eyes and stared at it, and then I felt it move in my hands as it fell to the left and to the right, as if the cat were bored. I began to laugh, and I looked at the ladies, who nodded and smiled. Minerva appeared beside me, but I could not take my eyes off of the cat's tail. Then it moved again and Minerva said, "You didn't really believe in the operation did you?"

I felt as if I were being exposed for weakness of faith in a fundamentalist church.

"No," I confessed, "I was really fascinated by the idea of the Incarnation, and I like your dad and all that, but this changes everything, I mean, my God! This thing really works!"

She was looking at me quizzically and I told her that I had dreamed all my life for an opportunity to witness a miracle of science, to be a part of something truly revolutionary in technology, and that I felt like I was in a dream.

Minerva said, "Hmm."

We stared into each other's eyes for a long time. It was as if she where used to this sort of activity and was amused at how excited I was that this Incarnation thing was not a giant hoax after all. The sisters and widows of the Chief told Minerva that the cat had been awake for a few hours, and was recovering well ahead of schedule. They were ready to begin the "exercising" phase of the operation. I thought I saw seeds in the water surrounding the leopard. They turned out be the ant heads that we had used as sutures. When I inspected the wound site, I could see the milky skin and the blue-black scar, and I could also see the pinholes left by the tiny mandibles. The hair stubble around the scar was getting thick. Fascinating. Some men arrived with a tarp lashed between poles, which I thought was a hammock. It turned out to be filled with water from the river. They slowly poured the water along the sides of the jaguar-Chief and a lot of milky crud swirled into view. We began to bail out the pit into buckets. We carried away the old water and fresh water arrived again. We did this regularly all day long. The entire tribe took turns carrying fresh water to the pit and bailing out the "used" water, which was a filmy layer of coagulated stuff on the surface. They were singing the songs and exercising the cat. This last task consisted of massaging the wound site and manipulating the animal's legs to simulate running. Someone had to hold the cats' head above water.

Throughout the day I got to take turns at making the cat "run" in the water. At first, I had to do all the work, and it almost felt as if rigor mortis were setting in, but every turn after that it got easier and easier, and towards the end of the day I could feel the cat swimming in the pit, and his tail wagged like a snake. I was in ecstasy. People fed me and I did have to take a few nature breaks, but for the most part, I witnessed the entire renaissance of a corpse into a living being. Throughout the day I had plenty of time to marvel at the impact this Incarnation would have on the world, on the rich and their endless plastic surgery routines and liposuction, their vitamins and personal trainers, their endless search for youth itself. I knew that this would only be available to the ultra-wealthy for a long time to come.

Minerva fed me information and food. The information was great. I ate smoked spider-monkey meat and fried grubs (mercifully, Mina fed me this without telling me what it was) and told me the reason the tribe had decided to share their secrets.

Grubs taste like tofu or mushrooms.

According to Chief Eight Jaguar, their jungle-world was being dissolved around its edges by civilization, and experiencing the flattening effect of "large peoples" on the earth. They knew that the plants and spiders and tree bark and all the other stuff needed for the Incarnation would become protected species, and their precious byproducts would become commodities only if the process could be marketed appropriately. The grand counsel of Chiefs had decided that if the governments of Mexico, Honduras, and Belize could be persuaded to designate the area a protected zone, then the Yohimbe and other indigenous people of the Yucatan Peninsula could save their habitat and their culture.

Eight Jaguar announced to the council that he was preparing for an Incarnation of his own and he proposed Elvin Williams as a candidate to be their agent to bring the process to the attention of the world. Many of the other Chiefs had met Elvin in his search for Eight Jaguar, and they thought he was crazy, but they also knew that he was a medicine man of his own culture.

They had met Minerva as well, when she was a child. The Chiefs agreed that Elvin could be ideal for the job, and in the end, it was his persistence that did it. They realized that he had devoted his entire life to his dream of finding their secret. They smoked marijuana that they got by trading with the campesinos, and laughed about Elvin's sunburn.

"That was two months ago," Minerva concluded. I asked her if she thought that the natives liked Elvin because of her.

"Well, I did have to translate for him many times, and sometimes I had to change what he said so that they would not kill him."

I then asked a question that suddenly popped into my head. I did not expect her to have an answer, but she did. I asked her how the people of the forest invented the Incarnation. She got excited as she told the story.

"About three hundred years ago, a legion of renegade Spaniards left their ship and captain in search of gold. These men risked hanging for their desertion, but they were ruthless in their hunt for riches. Their method was to go into a village and demand gold. When they felt that the natives were not forthcoming with the proper amount, or if the natives claimed to have none at all, then the conquistadors would chop the head off a young man, a *hunter*, and threaten to decapitate the Chief. Unfortunately, the distant relatives of the Jaguar clan had no gold. They knew that the conquistadors were in the area. The conquistadors had local mercenary guides, dogs, horses and guns. The Yohimbe attempted to raise tribute money, and were unable to. So they lost two young men and their Chief before the evil bastards left."

"Fortunately, their Chief, who was very wise and old and frail, had developed a special plan to be used as a last resort. Pre-selected members of the tribe carried the decapitated bodies and the heads into the forest, and the rest of the tribe scattered. They had hidden their next camp in several smaller hiding spaces, and the men with the corpses formed a tiny group that attempted to keep the Chief alive. The Chief's body was old and frail. They began by immersing his head in a pool of water. Then they brought the body of one of the stronger young men up to the throat of the old man and they literally held the two parts together, performing rudimentary CPR. In this way, the Chief's life was maintained for a few days. During this time, he supposedly had some important dreams, which supposedly led to the pirates being captured, by the captain they had deserted, their bloody treasure being forfeited and their eventual hanging.

"So they actually had discovered a rudimentary form of the Incarnación. The Chief was able to give his apprentices information to use in further development of this stunning new technique, and the tribe actually experimented on generations of Chiefs, until the damned thing actually worked, and could be used regularly!"

I suppose many Yohimbe gave their lives developing this technique.

Chapter 8: the Beast Recovers

As night fell, we were preparing to pull the beast out of the plasma and complete the rehabilitation process on dry land. As I remember it, the ladies began pulling on the cat's waterlogged flesh, which seemed to stretch, then some young boys got into the pit and pushed up on the panther.

As the cat lay on its side panting, I remember watching its eyes. The pupils had excellent sensitivity and he could track a branch with an ember on it as I waved it slowly before his face. He also twitched in response to loud noises. I looked into his eyes and wondered if there was still a person in there, or if all that was gone, washed down the river with the dead skin cells, the fur and the lumps of blood that had coagulated in the operation pit. Or in the ashes of the Chief's pyre. The beast woke up after sleeping for three hours. It was around two in the morning. I had stayed awake, talking with Mark and Carl about the operation. Carl proclaimed that we would all be rich soon, but Mark was remarkably quiet for once. We crowded near the ladies as they fed strips of meat to the Jaguar Chief. The cat ate continuously for an hour, about seven pounds of meat. Then he became active, and tried to stand up. We put wood on the fire so we could see what was going on.

At around four thirty a.m., the cat was finally able to get up. He paced around the fire ring slowly as if he were soaking up the heat of the flames. Someone tossed a handful of tobacco leaves onto the fire and they belched up a great cloud of white smoke, enveloping the great leopard. The cat tried to walk backwards to escape the acrid fumes, but he tripped on his own tail and fell and began to howl piteously. Mark and I were nearby and we sprang up and grabbed the beast to pull it free of the smoke. The cat began to writhe and struck at us, and actually cut Mark badly across the back of the arm. Then the smoke cleared, and the jaguar looked at Mark, and I swear, the spark of recognition flashed between them. Mark got up and went to take care of his arm. I offered to do it, and he looked at me, gave me a tired wave and said, "That's all right, Victor, I can get it done for free here," and wandered towards a group of Yohimbe, holding his arm. When I turned back to look at the jaguar, the cat was asleep on the mats. I listened to his chest, took his pulse and stared at the giant feline Jaguar-Chief. I was so tired that I lay down next to the beast.

Minerva draped a blanket over me. I wanted to bathe, and eat, and be in Minerva's tent, but the warmth of the blanket nourished me to sleep and I dreamed of Chief Eight Jaguar, a black panther with feathers of birds coming out of his fur and the face of an old human shaman, who told me that I had to marry Minerva and raise babies with her and showed me an ordinary house with a yard of nice grass, covered with thousands of wiggling, pink, cooing, happy babies.

Eight Jaguar told me to stop thinking of my body as a single living thing, but as lots of tiny living things. In my dream, he was dressed like a surgeon in an operating room gown. "Like a forest, all the parts of your body are alive and form the whole. Your experience of spirit is the sensation of all of the spirits within all of the billions of cells that compose your body. Every tiny cell has its own tiny flame of life. Your medicine teaches you that only a body can have a soul, but that is not true, a disease can have a soul, even though it is only made of tiny cells, but remember, each one has a spirit, just like you! A disease without a body can have a spirit, and you are not an individual, you are many tiny spirits, all put together. See how they can come apart, and go back together."

The next day I woke up to the sound of whispering and crying. I later had it explained to me by Mark, who told me that the wives of the Chief all slept in one area, and right around dawn one of the

Chief's wives woke up with the cat licking her face. The other wives then all wanted the cat to kiss them too, and they began hugging and pulling at him, but the beast became hostile and ran into the jungle, limping a little and making a lot of noise, for a jaguar   – or, for that matter a Yohimbe. The women sat around and talked for a while, and listened to the forest. Then, as if on some silent cue, the tribe began to strike camp. Youngsters rounded up all the animals that roamed around and tied them nose to tail, and then tied packs onto them, even the pigs, which was amazing to me because they put up with it. The men disassembled the posts that held up the thatched roofs and the women rolled up the food they had into the mats, and strapped them onto their backs. Water was collected into jugs that went onto reed and leather frames so they could be dragged.

At this time it became apparent that every single pair of legs carried some bundle of material. Leaves, fruit, baskets of frogs, branches full of caterpillars, webs and cocoons, hammocks packed with flowers. I was bewildered at the speed at which all this was happening. I went to Minerva's tent. She was speaking Spanish on a cellular phone and writing on a laptop computer, and did not stop when she saw me, but smiled. I went looking for Mark and Carl.

I found them packing Mark's notes, videotapes and laptop computer into a crate that also contained canisters packed with specimens of flowers, leaves, spiders and samples of river water, soil, even the ants used as sutures. I asked if Mark would need his computer for the trip home and Carl told me that it would not be necessary.

I looked at Mark and Carl said, "He's going native on us."

I was confused, and Mark nodded.

"Yeah, I don't want to go back to the States, man, I want to stay here with the real people."

(The name Yohimbe means "Real People"…as opposed to animals, I guess.)

We were all silent and I was wondering what would be an appropriate question to ask.

Are you really sure? Do you need anything? What if you change your mind?"

"Don't worry about me, Victor, this is what I've wanted all along"

But as I looked at Mark I saw a very sad, but also deliriously happy look in his eye, and I felt as if he had already vanished into the woods, with the natives. He was just as anxious as the clan was about the Incarnation and the way it turned out, and he empathized with their situation more than that of Elvin Williams.

I said, "I would like to see you again someday."

Carl told me that Mark was taking a GPS transmitter with him so we could find him again in the future.

"Gimme at least a couple years before you start looking for me, alright?"

Carl said, "OK," smiled, turned, and walked away. Not a very emotional parting. Mark casually handed me about one hundred of the curved obsidian scalpels, all tied in a neat bag. I was startled that I had completely forgotten to procure these indispensable tools of the Incarnation, and I thanked him in a sudden and embarrassing rush of feelings, then I sort of stood there, turning red. Mark told me that the emotional rushes come with having Chief Eight Jaguar "running loose in your head."

Then Minerva appeared among us.

"So you are snubbing civilization, hm?"

"You got to live with them, Minerva," Mark pointed out.

There was a loud pop behind us, followed by a loud hissing noise. It was the children inflating one of the rafts we had brought to escape the jungle in. The rafts had compressed air cartridges in them and Carl had shown the children how to pull on the red cord "tongue" to discharge the air. The Yohimbe had been waiting to see the boats we had. The fact that they got so much bigger than the boxes they were packed in really affected them and they laughed hysterically, with huge eyes, as the kids inflated all of four of them. And they decided that someone had pulled Carl's cord to make him get big. An old lady pushed on his stomach and whistled loudly like the sound of the inflating boats. I liked that. Carl seemed to like it too.

We tied the boats all together into a long fleet, and loaded each boat with samples, backpacks, and other equipment. I asked about the parachute, and Mark told me that the Yohimbe will take it. Everything fit without needing the last boat at all. Mark decided that the Yohimbe could deflate the raft and keep it. The fleet was then secured to a tree. Minerva took one last walk around the camp and picked up a dead battery, a book, and some other trash. Po-Asu approached and gave me a snakeskin bag. It had a cord on it and could be worn around the neck, like his. I attempted to open the bag, but it was sewn shut. I asked him what was in it, and he shook his head and indicated that I just leave the bag shut. I put the thing around my neck and dropped the snakeskin bag under my shirt. People were watching. I did not want to be rude again.

I said, "Thank you" and he answered me, "You're welcome," mimicking my voice nicely. We smiled at each other. Then the boy Po-Asu straightened up, and turned to Minerva. He gave her a scroll, then he ran into the woods. It was the "what's inside a girl?" scroll. She hugged it and watched the little monkey-boy disappear, and she was crying.

I shook hands with Mark.

Minerva hugged Mark, still crying, and she whispered something small in his ear.

Then we all looked at the Yohimbe. They were thinning out, slipping into the jungle, waving goodbye like people do all over the world. Minerva said to Mark, "You'd better go..." and we all smiled at each other. Mark turned and jogged into the woods to catch up with his new friends. And as they left, it was like watching a ship sail away from a dock, with someone you know on it. The jungle became very quiet. Carl and I looked at each other and then at Minerva, who was untying the rafts and getting into the last one. We followed, looking at our footprints as they led into the water. We began to drift toward the Atlantic Ocean. We slipped away from the flat rock where Minerva and I had made love. We passed the place where we had gathered water for the operation, and we were surrounded by the sweet river, and the jungle rolled over the banks like a giant carpet, and the low branches of trees dragged their leaves in the water, with slimy weeds trailing.

Chapter 9: The Laboratory of Dr. Williams

After a few hours of drifting, we came to a very wide spot in the river, and Carl paddled our flotilla toward a tiny island in the middle. Minerva tied our rope to a tree branch that hung out over the water, and the raft chain slowly swung around, with us under the shade of the tree and the cargo rafts stretching out down the river. Carl got a case full of electronics from the boat behind ours and produced satellite phone and a radio beacon transmitter. He began speaking Spanish, and was laughing, nodding his head, saying; "si!   si!" Minerva had the Global Positioner and read off our location in degrees and minutes to Carl, who translated them into the phone.

Carl put down the phone and lay back in the sun, in heaven. Minerva picked up the telephone and dialed a long number, looking at me. She said, "Hi dad!" and began talking about our location in the river, looking around. Then she told her father that Mark had decided to stay with the Yohimbe, which they discussed for a while, and then she handed me the phone.

I cleared my throat. I looked at Minerva as if she could give me a hint. I put the phone up to my ear and said "Hello?"

"Well congratulations, Doctor Germaine! You did it! Minerva tells me that the damned beast survived!"

"He did indeed, sir!" I said.

"This is fantastic!"

"I have only seen the cat limping"

"Yes, yes, my boy, but the miracle has happened, and I feel confident that you can duplicate the results for me upon our return."

"Yes, Dr. Williams, I can, and by the way, you sound fantastic."

88

"I feel fantastic, now that I have spoken to Mina and you."
I told Elvin about the dream I had with Chief Eight Jaguar. Elvin said, "Wow" and was silent for a moment. I tuned out the world to hear what he was going to say next. He asked me to take a handful of river water and drink it. I did it. He asked me to describe it.
I said, "Sort of velvety, like peach juice. Sweet and warm."
Elvin said, "Thank you, Victor."
Then Elvin spoke with Carl, who actually woke up for the occasion. After Carl turned off the phone it was quiet again.
We watched an iguana swimming in the water, and some beautiful parrots flew overhead. I looked at the small island we were tied to. It was a long dark rock with vegetation growing out of the crevices in it. The tree we were tied to had a twisting mass of roots that went into a series of holes in the rock. I looked closer. A very straight row of holes. I slowly asked the two with me to come and look at the rock. When we all redistributed ourselves in the boat, Carl reached out and touched the rock. He laid his hand on it and stared at the thing for a long time.
"Well. This is a German submarine, of W.W.II vintage,"
he said with comical nonchalance.
It really took a few minutes of disbelief before we could comprehend the coincidence of drifting, on our way out of the jungle, to the very place that Elvin had searched for so many years ago.
I asked Minerva, "Do you think this is the same one…"
Minerva was on the phone again. Soon we were all taking turns describing to Elvin what we saw, which in reality, was not that much.
When I spoke to him he said, "Victor, this is a sign."
I agreed and we all were elated with the sense that something very rare and strange was happening. Minerva tied a transmitter to the tree and told me it could go for another year if it did not get destroyed. "Maybe after the Incarnation, dad will want to come see this thing for himself."
I told her that when Elvin originally told me the story, the bit about the submarine was actually nearly as unbelievable as that nonsense about an "Incarnación."
"He's been telling me about this stupid thing all my life!" she laughed.

89

I climbed onto the hulk and saw that it was covered with rust and bits of rotten wooden planking. I broke off a bit of this rotten wood for a souvenir for Elvin, and we unpacked the video camera to shoot it. Then just as the silence was humming again, we heard the arrival of the helicopter. It cleared the forest behind us and the size of it was startling. This helicopter was much bigger that the one I had come to the jungle in, and it had a bottom like a boat, with small pontoons on each side. It landed in the river downstream of us and kicked up a massive cloud of water. The pilot idled the engines and motioned us to advance as the blades slowed. We untied the rafts and drifted toward the helicopter as a crewmember opened the side cargo door and tossed an anchor into the river. The rotors swung overhead like a giant fan and produced the first breeze I had felt in what seemed like an eternity. We paddled over and grabbed the rail on the side of the aircraft. Carl and I began lugging the crates up to the guy in the cargo bay, who took long looks into the jungle and at us as he worked. Getting the rafts deflated and bundled into cargo nets for storage on the helicopter came next. Minerva was telling the pilot about the submarine and the pilot was smiling and shaking his head as he looked at the tiny island in the stream. The crewman winched up the anchor line and clamped the anchor to the side of the cargo bay. The door slid shut, the engines throttled up, the rotors began to shred the sky, and we lifted off of the surface of the water. We rose high above the river, hovered for a moment and looked down at the submarine. Since we knew what it was, and had a view of it from above, we could appreciate the full mass of it, its nose rising out of the murky water, covered with vegetation, and about twenty feet away, its conning tower just visible under the velvety surface. Minerva shot more video of it.

It was too loud to talk comfortably in the helicopter, so we just looked at each other in amazement. Then we turned away and began the long ride home. There was a long bench running around the inside of the cargo area, and I reclined onto one and slept easily in the roaring, lurching machine.

We flew for about six hours and landed in a city in central Mexico,

I don't remember which one. We transferred directly onto a small private jet and were in the air so quickly that I wondered if all the cargo had been loaded. It was becoming dark and we were fed fantastic boxed lunches of soda and sandwiches. It tasted perfect after days of smoked mystery meat, and I looked at Carl, who was chewing slowly, with his eyes shut. Compared to the helicopter, the jet was silent, and we all soon had our seats reclined and were falling asleep. Minerva was next to me and we held hands, and I looked at her hand carefully and loved the very sight of her. She fell asleep and I continued to look at her. Then I followed her to sleep. I dreamed of a wedding in a church. Floating above the altar, I saw myself and Minerva there smiling at each other. Elvin Williams was the priest, and the Yohimbe filled the pews, the white carpet had muddy footprints all over it and it was covered with every imaginable sort of bug and reptile, and I tried not to move my feet so that I would not step on anything and instead of being terrified by the sight of the creatures, I found the sight of them soothing.

We woke up in San Diego and passed through customs as if I was under some sort of sedation. I remember people around us staring at our muddy clothes, our oily hair. We had bathed, but we probably had really bad body odor. Smoke and sweat. We were driven to a series of clinics along a cliff overlooking the ocean. We approached a gated entrance to the side of one of the modern buildings and a guard motioned us in, but looked us over suspiciously as we drove past. Before we had even stopped rolling, Minerva opened the door and was running into the clinic. We followed her into a door, down some stairs, past another guard station, and into the most opulent and high tech laboratory I have ever seen. The site of the modern Incarnación. It was a state-of-the-art medical research lab, and then some. The main room was large. Vast. It was filled with a mixture of art, antiques and modern equipment. There were professional reproductions of masterpiece paintings hanging on the walls, large Persian carpets on the floor, and gothic lamp sconces with flickering bulbs warmed the fluorescent light that glowed from the ceiling.

It looked as if it were someone's home. There was a TV set,

books, newspapers and remains of a meal on a table. I then figured out that I was walking into someone's living room. Elvin's home.

Besides the fancy accouterments, the area was also filled with some of the most expensive laboratory and test equipment I have ever seen. I get lab supply catalogs in the mail and I sometimes I actually read them. There was also a custom-made piece, right in the middle of the room. A giant, clear plastic tub the size of a Jacuzzi, with mats and drains around it to catch spilled water. I stared at it for a long time. There was a small bedroom to one side. Elvin sat on the bed happily hugging his daughter; and I just looked around.

"Welcome to my lab, Dr. Germaine! It's nice to see you again, and you too, Carl!"

Elvin smiled at Carl and me, and we walked over to him to shake his hand.

I thanked him for inviting me into his cozy little lab. I noticed that he had lost some of the grip he had when I first met him, and I sensed that he had experienced a close brush with death while we were gone.

"They put someone's aortic valve in my heart."

"I'm glad to see it is working sir, but… you won't need it much longer."

"Good! Good!" he said.

We assembled in the laboratory, and Carl introduced me to the "Biological Lab Director," one Doctor Avery Jones. The truck carrying our samples had arrived just after us, and we began unpacking the material. Some of it went directly into a refrigerator. The interns had apparently been working with other samples of the medicines from an earlier shipment, and the ones we brought were the ones with the shortest shelf lives. Minerva had described the work that was going on while we were in the jungle. "Avery has been studying and synthesizing the various plant and animal solutions in preparation for the big operation." Avery looked at me as if he recognized me and told me he wanted to hear all about the dream journey Chief Eight Jaguar had taken me on. The other lab personnel listened while Carl and Minerva went to take showers. I told Dr. Avery and the others about the vision of the molecules unzipping themselves, the skin coming apart, the nerve ends washing away, the artificial water-plasma in the pit supporting the cells as if it was blood. Avery told me that most of it he understood, and had been able to replicate in the lab, but that something was in the river water that he could not figure out. His theory was that there was something in the water at certain times of the year, a seasonal plant pollen, or a migratory fish by product.

We unpacked the bottles of river water. The technicians in the lab divided up the samples and began to test it in different machines, one of which I recognized as a beautiful and super-expensive Nelson-Downing gas chromatograph spectrometer, used to determine exact amounts of elements in a solution. I had always wanted one of those. Another assistant poured samples into test tubes and put these into small steel "buckets" that fit into a large Swedish Colden A334 centrifuge. He closed the brushed aluminum lid, locked it, balanced the machine, and started the motor. It began to spin at an incredible rate; the samples in it whirring like a solid disk. Minerva wandered over to me and said that she wanted to do the operation as soon as possible. I agreed, and I stated that it was time for me to know who the host body for this operation would be. She hung her head low. She slowly led me to a darkened room, and turned on the lights, revealing a hospital bed with a young man lying in it. He looked like a corpse with respirators and tubes connected to him.

"Who is this guy?" I asked. Minerva sat near the patient's foot, and petted the sleeping one's shin.

"He was my cousin. He overdosed on a mixture of amphetamines and heroin last spring at a party in his fraternity. He actually collapsed on top of a girl he was having sex with on the balcony."

I was appalled.

She did not show disdain.

"Amphetamines and heroin?" I asked.

"That was typical for Henry...he didn't know whether he was coming or going...the sad thing is that he might have survived if he had stuck with either one or the other."

I looked at this young party animal, unable to wake up, dreaming of nothing, sugar water dripping into his arm, and his watery pee trickling down a catheter into a bottle that hung from a hook under his bed. Pathetic.

I asked Minerva what Elvin was planning on doing before his nephew so conveniently scrambled his own egg.

"Oh, he was going to purchase a corpse and simply risk rejection."

I was shocked by her frankness.

"I was unaware that a decent fresh corpse was so easy to come by."

"They come from the same place where the cadavers you practiced surgery on in school came from, they are just more expensive, and the availability is limited, especially since Elvin is an O-negative."

"He is?"

She nodded. "They tattoo a serial number on your foot and give you a lump sum of money. When you die, they collect and sell your body. There are many healthy young people out there with the tattoo, and we still receive notification from brokers with good candidates for our study about once a month."

"What exactly is a 'good candidate'?"

"Well, he has to be the right blood type, the same height, and near death due to an injury to the back of the head."

"Near death?" I squinted.

"Well, when a family of, say, a victim of a motorcycle accident, wants to pull the plug on their kid, the organ recovery team intervenes and keeps the body alive until they have matched the organs with recipients, then they can all be harvested and delivered at once."

"We simply plan on keeping the patient alive until the operation."

"But don't they want to watch their loved ones pass on?" I asked.

"Not all of them, but yes, they usually do. In our plan, as soon as he flat-lines, we would wheel him out quickly, saying that he had to go to be dissected. They never follow. Then we simply resuscitate to revive the patient." She made it sound so obvious.

"Revive them back to their coma?"

"Duh, and remember, this only works with families that plan on cremation and no viewing of the corpse." She counted these last two points on her fingers, and almost made it sound feasible.

My interest in the subject was exhausted, but to this day I wonder how the Incarnación would affect future donations for transplant purposes, if it had become as common as Elvin had planned. To tell a bereaved family that their son's kidneys or corneas could help someone else is one thing, but to tell some mother that her child will be walking around soon, but would not recognize her, is quite another. Impossible. I asked Minerva about the risk of rejection. She reported to me that Glaxinol, a new grafting compound, was developed by a subsidiary of Elvin's company working with plant material found in the Yohimbe rainforest.

"It has remarkable anti-rejection properties. They used it on his heart, as a matter of fact."

"Cool," said I.

Avery stepped into the room and told us that as soon as the centrifuge was done and the final analysis of the river water could be performed, we could begin the operation. I asked for a time and he said about an hour, if his theory was correct, but if he was wrong, then he had no idea when he would be ready. I was hungry and we decided to call out for pizza because they guarantee fast delivery. Upstairs there was a locker room with showers and towels, robes and fresh clothing for us. I showered, scrubbed my hair, and suited up in a lab coat that matched the rest of the crew's coats. The lab coat had my name embroidered on it, and the courtesy that demonstrated made me feel really welcome in this new group. The technicians all gathered around the tank in the middle of the room and filled it with warm distilled water from bottles. We ate pizza. Bill, the youngest of our group, at twenty, took the temperature of the water in the tub. In a flash, I recalled the image of Minerva monitoring the temperature in the clay pit during the Incarnation, although I could not remember actually seeing her do it, which seemed strange.

The tank was clear plastic, about three feet deep and five feet per side. It was built low on the floor and was surrounded by a rubber mesh pad to keep us off the water we would inevitably spill during the operation. I wished to Carl that we had brought some of the mats that the Jungle people had made. Aside from the pretty decorator objects, all around me was a conventional laboratory, with its filtered air, even lighting, and the smell of sterile objects in the delicate paper wrappers they come in. It was weird because at that particular moment, the trip I had just returned from sort of rushed through me, and I felt like I was walking out of a theater after watching a long movie. In a compressed burst of images I remembered many little things about the Yohimbe that I had not really thought about in the moment, like the way they were always holding hands, and the way that they all slept in hammocks, and often just lay in them watching the day go by. A father, a mother, a baby, all tucked into a hammock with their small round faces peering out, smiling. Avery began to add powders and liquids to the water and the tank had a milky fog billowing through it. I felt the side of the tank. It was almost hot.

A pump began to circulate the water and a row of tiny holes in the tank's floor released billions of tiny bubbles into the solution, and I watched them swirling around. We heard a beep and the centrifuge began to slow down. When it stopped, Chandrath took out the samples and passed them around. Avery put the sample into a box, which contained a small camera. The sample was lit from behind, and a monitor revealed an enlarged image of it. The centrifuge had compressed the sediment in the tube into a series of different colored bands, with the heaviest material at the bottom. Avery told me that all the earlier samples of river water had the same stratified layers of sediment in it, but that the sample we had brought with us had a layer of a new material in it that he had not seen before. It was gray, and it constituted a tiny percent of the material in the test tube. It was right on top.

"Something very light, and it probably evaporates very quickly," Chandrath said.

A syringe was clamped onto the box over the sample; a needle was lowered into the test tube, into the region of the gray band of

EIGHT JAGUAR

mystery substance. The tiny specimen was vacuumed up. The material was squirted onto a slide and placed into the chamber of a shiny new Fuji-Shinden Tunneling Electron Microscope, a compact prototype unit that I was not familiar with. I was fascinated by the power of its magnification displayed on the flat screen monitor. It could probably see quarks and leptons. Avery asked Chandrath to engage the false color synthesizer. We looked at the abstract art on the screen of the microscope's large monitor. They seemed to recognize it, and Carl whispered tentatively,

"It is a… spore, or the remains of a spore from a tree that rots at certain times of the year, and puts this stuff in the water. We actually have a flask of it and can use it to fully replicate the conditions in the river during the operation."

I asked what it did. Carl was trying to answer the question but he was unable to and just mumbled quietly.

Chandrath looked up. "We haven't the faintest idea what it does."

I smiled. "So that's everything?"

Carl said, "Yep."

I noticed that Minerva was looking at me apprehensively: "Well, maybe not everything…"

Minerva had been, until that moment, the very picture of confidence and savoir-faire. When I looked at her I sensed apprehension. Her forehead was pressed into a cute and pleading brow. I arched my brow and stared at her and she told me to step into the next room. There was a small office and we left the lights off as we walked in. There was a window from the office, looking into Elvin's room. We stood next to each other for a moment watching at him as he spoke with Carl. Minerva began slowly. "Do you remember your first night in the jungle?"

I nodded.

"Then you remember the Chief asking you if you had exorcised the body of the host."

I told her that I remembered that too.

"Well Victor, I have to confess that I don't know if we have completely accomplished this, or how to, or even if it is truly necessary

97

to the successful outcome of the operation."

I turned to her, my mouth was open and I was silent. I had to think about this. I had not considered the Chief's question until this very moment. I finally asked her how it could be possible that she could have grown up around the Yohimbe and not have learned about the exorcism. She told me that the exorcism was always performed far from the clan to protect them from the ghost that the ritual would inevitably produce, and that the details were *never* discussed.

"I don't think that Chief Eight Jaguar could conceive of a culture that did not include people capable of knowing how to exorcise a body of an unwanted spirit."

I asked her what she thought was the best thing to do.

"Look, in case you have not noticed, Elvin is not a very spiritual man, and he does not believe that there is "anyone home" in his nephew's body. To a man like Elvin, the technical aspects of the operation are the only relevant consideration."

I asked her if she thought "anyone was home."

"Well I have no way of really knowing, do I?" She distractedly brushed her hair back off her face.

"I asked Mark to come on this expedition to try and learn how to do an exorcism, but he never could get the Chief to teach it to him. In fact, the Chief told us that Mark already knew how to do it, but Mark seemed to have no idea what the Chief was talking about, and I feel that that is why he did not want to return with us —either he was ashamed of not completing his mission, or he has become obsessed with the goal of learning the secret of the exorcism himself."

I took a deep breath and asked Minerva how, in her opinion, we could take the Incarnación out of the jungle, out of context, eliminate one step in the process, and expect to get the desired results. "I wonder if Eight Jaguar would have let us in on his little secret here if he knew that we don't really believe his bogeyman Gods exist, that we just want to steal his cool trick and use it on ourselves."

I was pointing towards the hydro-pneumatic-electric-sterilized plastic pool in the next room; the one that would be our substitute for the pit in the clay that I was acquainted with. I actually felt angry with Minerva and I was not ready to feel that because I was also falling in love with her, and while this sensation was not new to me, I had been unaware that it could occur so quickly, or be so disorienting. I left the little office and walked into the room where Elvin and Carl were talking. Minerva followed me closely, speaking my name.

Carl and Elvin turned to us and I interrupted them. "Is it true that we do not know how to exorcise the body of the host?"

There was a decent and pregnant silence in the room as the four of us looked at each other. No one knew what to say and I wondered out loud what else we might be overlooking.

Elvin spoke with calm authority, "Victor, have you ever heard of the Tibetan book of the dead?"

I looked around at the little crowd that was forming and asked him what he was talking about, and he continued, "The wisdom of the Tibetans scares the shit out of the Chinese Communists, and the Buddhists there believe that they have, in their *Book of the Dead,* a record of the soul's journey through the afterlife."

I was amused. Elvin continued, "They believe that when someone dies, you should sit near the head of the corpse and speak into the ear of the dead one, and announce yourself to it, and literally tell the dead person that he or she is dead! And then they read this *Book of the Dead* to the deceased, in order to guide them on their journey to reincarnation, or to ascend into heaven, or whatnot."

He seemed proud of himself for having proved that this whole concept of a spirit that survives death could be codified in an instruction manual. In a way his odd arrogance reminded me of that of Chief Eight Jaguar, and I smiled. I think Carl was smiling too. I told Elvin that I most definitely thought that the Tibetan idea was a good one and if it was the least we could do, we should do it. I asked Minerva if the Chief had exorcised the jaguar in the jungle.

She said, "Hey! I think he might have, right there in front of us, and I videotaped it!"

Mina rummaged through a crate of videotapes, and we queued up a tape, and forwarded it to a section of the Chief petting the sleeping cats' head, and we turned up the volume. Through the background noise of the jungle, the Chief was singing softly to the giant leopard, and we noticed that he was singing into the animal's twitching ear. I turned to look at Elvin, who met my eyes and shrugged, because he could not translate it. We turned to Minerva, and she listened for a while. "It is not in the Yohimbe language, nor is it one of Eight Jaguar's trance voices. I think it might be a totemic voice related to the Jaguar's growl. He may have been speaking Jaguarese."

Elvin said he loved the idea of "Jaguarese," adding that the nephew was not Catholic, so a conventional exorcism was out of the question. He got out of his bed, trailing his catheters and IV pole (held by Chandrath). The ancient millionaire hobbled out of the bedroom, crossed the laboratory, and stepped into the room with pale ligh shining on the pale body. Elvin rubbed the light switch and watched the lights gradually illuminate Henry's almost albino complexion. Then he stooped in front of a chair, and dragged it to the side of the boy, sat heavily into it and inhaled. We followed Elvin into the room and all gathered around the bed. Elvin leaned back, closed his eyes, and pronounced his mock exorcism as a matter of fact:

"I, Elvin Gettysburg Williams, do hereby claim this here inert human body as my property, and state to all within the sound of my voice that I intend to take up permanent residence within this body and am thus compelled to order that any present inhabitant please vacate the aforementioned body immediately!"

He laughed briefly and looked at his daughter with a twinkle in his eye.

"Maybe I can try a kinder, gentler exorcism for the sake of Mr. Germaine." He looked at me.

I said, "By all means sir…"

Elvin took the limp hand of the young man in his own wrinkled claw and placed his other hand on top of it, invoking the image of a priest, and attempted to look very holy. He shouted "Young man! HEY! YOU! Oh what was it… Oh I remember: Henry Davis Nelson! I'm sorry to tell you this but you are for all intents and purposes *dead*, son. I don't think you deserved to die, but if you were listening to your friends and family over the last year or so, you have heard all of them saying goodbye to you! If you're still in there, GET OUT! It's closing time, and a new renter is movin' on in. I don't know where you are supposed to go, but I have read that if you see a beautiful bright white light, go to that!"

He breathed a few times and continued. "Failing that, climb inside the next lotus blossom you happen to see, and bon voyage, baby! Now I really think you must move on."

He got up and shuffled back to his room and told Chandrath to put "the drug" into the IV channel. He laid back onto his bed, took a deep breath, smiled at Minerva, and said, "See you soon!" and slowly fell asleep as the technicians left the room to prepare for the Incarnation.

Chapter 10:
The Incarnation of Elvin Williams

Elvin had brought to a close my last reservation about the operation, or at least exonerated me of any personal responsibility, and I was beginning to anticipate meeting the new Elvin, to ask him what it is like to be clothed in a brand new body. I marveled thus as I gazed at the old and new corpses lying on lowered gurneys, next to each other in the lab. The crew of lab assistants was composed of three surgeons: Drs. Feenburg, Sales, and Vaughn. We discussed the obsidian blades, which I distributed, and a few technical tips for the crucial incisions. We fast-forwarded the Incarnación tape on the VCR, and I stopped at the parts where the various nerve tissues were swabbed with different solutions and spliced together, adding hints to help prepare the team. We all were excited, and even the hardest-boiled professionals among us were having a hard time hiding it.

And to make a long story short, we basically went through the operation as it had been done in the jungle. There were some differences, however, such as the smell. I asked Minerva if she noticed the lack of a smell, and after I described it to her, she told me that the smell I remember was the women steaming grubs in banana leaves. I told her that I missed it. She told me that she did too. The operation did go quickly, and the two spinal cords were almost the same exact size so I did not have to spend a lot of time making adjustments with the wedges. Elvin's general physique and especially his spine, was in remarkably good condition. He was supposedly a health nut, with a sophisticated vitamin and supplement regimen, and he exercised and did yoga every morning at dawn. We closed the wound with surgical staples, and that was a disappointment to me. I felt that we could have learned a lot about an alternative technology using the ants, which we actually had with us in a terrarium. But I was slightly intimidated by the other scientists because they were older and more experienced than I and they had already seen Elvin make an ass of me for wanting to perform an exorcism on someone in a coma. I decided that I could still use the ants for my own personal projects. Instead of a bucket brigade of barefoot children, we recharged the tank with fresh water by simply turning a handle on a valve connected to a water softening and filtration system. A row of small ports in the pipe going into the tub had apertures into which the 'rotten tree spore' was added, along with the other substances that would simulate the composition of the river water. The engineer who designed it was also one of the surgeons, Dr. Sales.

The fresh water rose slowly in the tank, and the swirling red debris lifted and drained through a hole near its rim, revealing the floating, breathing corpse of a young man. He had a tube coming out of his mouth and a bolt of orange and blue lightning tattooed down his back, over his ears and across his smooth brow. We all just stared at our experiment for a moment, and then I took off my shoes and socks, rolled up my pants, took off my lab coat, and stepped into the pit with my patient. I sensed an inner guidance, a compelling urge to act, similar to my experience during the Incarnación in the jungle.

The bottom of the tank was slippery.

"You need those textured flower decals on the bottom of the tub for traction, Dr Sales!"

"For the commercial units? Hey—I think that is a great idea!" he smiled at me, "I'll see that you collect royalties for your improvement."

"Thank you Dr. Sales, I just love money."

I felt like making the creature in the tank swim. Chandrath, the child prodigy student from Bombay, was the second to have his shoes off. I told him to match my rhythm and we did a sort of breaststroke with the patient, who was rigid. It took considerable effort to move him. That night I spent a lot of time in the pit, and my hands and feet became wrinkly.

I had a hard time trying to explain to the other surgeons the exact nature of the movements necessary to fully exercise the healing grafts. "Think of it as dancing," I told them.

"Think of it as a special form of golf swing," Minerva added, at just the right moment.

We exercised the patient for hours, watching the bubbles rising around his head. It eventually got easier to move his limbs, and eventually he began to feel like a living thing. As it had done in the jungle, the scar on the patient's back was healing at a fantastic rate. There are varieties of bamboo that, when young, grow so fast that you can see it; I imagined that this was a similar phenomenon. While I was examining the suture site, I saw Minerva, kneeling beside the tank, looking through the plastic at the patient's face. I looked at her through the water, and although the water distorted and refracted her image and surrounded her with rippling iridescent rainbows, I could see her very well. She was crying. I stood up to look over the side of the tank, so that I could see her eyes, and I asked her what was wrong, and after a moment she told me that our patient's eyes were open.

"He's looking at me!" she shouted, with joy coloring her voice.

I looked at the form floating face down in the pool, and he was moving his hands, reaching. I put my hand into his and his fingers closed around mine and began pulling. At first I underestimated the recovering man's strength. I lost my footing in the aquarium and I almost toppled onto his wounded back. I managed to grab the edge of the tank and hold fast. Minerva and Dr. Sales were there in time to assist me and we managed to pull the patient into a sitting position in the water. We looked at his exhausted face and he began to wretch and cough. We held his face near the drain in the rim of the tank as he heaved up a volume of water. Then his gasping became a single word, delivered with tremendous effort, and we heard this first word spoken by the incarnation of Elvin Gettysburg Williams III:

"Pain."

I administered a reasonable bolus of Morphine and we rolled

Minerva's youthful father onto a stretcher, and put him into bed. We ordered more pizza and began to clean up the lab, and drain the tank. Minerva and another doctor placed electrodes on the sleeping re-Elvin, and hooked him up to a monitor, and began to analyze his condition. He seemed to be doing fine. Oddly enough, I had not noticed until then that he had undergone abdominal surgery, perhaps a few months ago. I asked Minerva about it.

"After his drug overdose, he needed a new liver—and he had a full blood transfusion, like the rock stars get so they don't have withdrawal symptoms."

I stared at the body, and I remembered talking to the old man only a week before. He had been wrinkly and feeble, but defiant. Now I realize d that he had been worried, and trying to hide it. Now, even in sleep, even under sedation, he wore the unmistakable countenance of vitality, and an irresistible rush of excitement filled me. I finally allowed myself to taste the indescribably sweet taste of the first acknowledgement of success. I hugged Minerva and she was as energized as I was. We smiled at each other and started happily giggling, and it spread through the place, and we all began laughing out loud. Chandrath got a Led Zeppelin song on the radio playing as we drank Champagne and ate left-over pizza. Minerva danced with me and led me down the hall...

I woke up in an empty bed. I could hear voices outside the door. I quickly dressed over my body odor and jogged barefoot into the laboratory. I instantly saw that both of the rooms that Elvin and his nephew had previously occupied were empty. I followed the sound of talking into a small kitchen. Everyone was sitting around the youthful Elvin, watching him eat cereal, listening to him crack jokes. Carl, Chandrath and Dr. Sales were sitting on the counter next to the microwave oven. Minerva was cooking omelets for breakfast. She was chopping bell peppers, avocado and tomatoes. I stepped into the room and I gazed into the perfectly normal looking eyes of the newest of the group. I asked him how he felt.

He said, "That, my good friend, I am happy to say, is no longer your concern!"

I smiled. He continued, "Have you forgotten that I am a doctor? Don't let looks deceive you, whipper-snapper! *I am still much older than you!*"

I smiled, and bent to a slight bow at the waist, saying, "Congratulations."

Life was as normal as it could be, for a about a week. We watched the new Elvin around the clock.

A married couple named Richard and Alice Moore, both doctors, spent all of their time writing articles for publication in the medical journals. This involved processing a vast amount of tedious process instructions, technical data, test results and definitions of terms, which is how we scientists take the fun out of describing miracles. They also began the work of preparing documents for the patent process. When Elvin was awake he was happy, alert and talkative. He described the long and detailed dream he had during the operation, saying that he had wandered through a dump, and was chased by a mob. He had passed many car accidents, and was terrified by the mutilated bodies he saw. He wondered why the bodies were left in the cars. Then he came to a park and was seduced by lovely women, who played expensive handmade acoustic guitars and smoked high -grade marijuana through colored glass pipes. They had a picnic of splendid food spread out over Persian carpets, and lounged on piles of silk cushions, under a paisley canopy.

He said that he stayed there for a long time but then saw a splendid lake, with large flowers floating on it. Although the ladies pleaded with him to stay, he left to go swim in the water. He was drawn irresistibly to the flowers, and suddenly found himself stuck inside one of them, and the flower was tight around him, and he found the pressure uncomfortable, and the flower filled with water, and he woke up drowning.

"This is pretty much how the Tibetan Book of the Dead describes it. So I guess that when you die, the best version of the afterlife you've got in your head is the version you get."

He told this in a deadpan voice that just fell into the silence of the room. As he talked, I ignored him and looked at the weird blue scars left by the staples. The scar looked like barbed wire, or perhaps a crown of thorns tattooed around his bald head. I listened to him confirm once and for all that he had *been* to the other side and its all been said and done before, and that it was not some shattering experience, that he was not a transformed man. So I told him as much.

"So it's pretty much as you expected?"

Elvin said, "Yep."

"But then, you never really did die, did you, I mean, isn't that the whole point of this operation, that you are afraid of death?"

Elvin looked at me with a filthy but winning smile and reminded me that I was now much closer to death than he. "By at least ten years!"

We laughed. I thanked him again for choosing me to do the operation.

"Oh, there was another guy."

"So why didn't he do it?"

"He cheated at cards!"

I flew back to Boston. I went straight to Mrs. P's apartment to check up on my cat. When the taxi dropped me off in front of my building I literally sniffed the air with homesick joy. Tux the cat was still asleep on top of Mrs. P's refrigerator. Mrs. P readily admitted that she was *worried* that I was back for good, and she wouldn't have Tux with her every day; so I told her that I might be moving to the West Coast, and I asked her if she would like to keep the cat. She became quite charming. We shook hands on it. I reached on top of the fridge, and petted my giant lazy cat for the last time. For some inscrutable reason, I felt a moment of sadness. It went away, and I left, after a moment of odd silence between Mrs. P and myself. I told my interns at my lab all about the Incarnación. They were floored. I had decided that I would try to include them in the project because they are a great team of specialists. They were stunned but excited, and I told them to think about it, and we would all know more after the release of the reports. Their initial response was very positive. Naturally, I advised them to keep the announcement secret. I spent a day reorganizing my life for a bi-coastal month or two.

That night I realized how much I had gotten used to sleeping next to a woman in the short time I had known Minerva. We called each other on the phone often, and I think my staff noticed it, as I heard someone refer to me as "Honey," as in, "Honey wants to know where the schedule is."

Chapter 11:
Meet William Ichabod Nelson

By the time I got back to San Diego the young Elvin had changed his name to William Ichabod Nelson, of all things, and was out shopping with the Drs. Moore and Chandrath.

"The new man has a real GQ consciousness," said Minerva, who stayed at the lab to meet me when I returned. She hugged me, and when I looked into her eyes, I knew the moment was right. I dropped to one knee, cleared my throat and presented her a small scallop shaped box from Marsden Jewelers, on Liberty Avenue. I said, "Minerva, I offer you my life in marriage."

I did not know what to say next. Minerva nodded her head yes. She opened the tiny box, looked at the ring with a flush of smiles, and took it out of its holder slowly, held it up and then put on the ring on her finger quickly, and hugged me for a long time, crying very softly. I held my fiancée in my arms and shut my eyes. When I opened my eyes, I was looking into the ring box that Minerva held. Because her arm was wrapped around my neck, the ring box was very close to my face, and slightly out of focus, and as we hugged and savored the moment of our engagement I looked into this dreamy, satiny, velvety shell and I heard the ocean.

The preposterous young William Ichabod Nelson charged into the room, followed by the others. He spoke way too loudly, and the reflective and shiny surfaces of the laboratory seemed to amplify him and I winced at the shrill tones of his voice.

Chandrath leaned to tell me that William seemed slightly hard of hearing, and not admitting it.

William Ichabod turned and said, "I heard that!"

"Mr. Ickybod reminds me of my cantankerous *old* dad," Minerva stated.

But William Ichabod Nelson was way beyond all that, and was stripping to the boxers and trying on different outfits, jackets, ties, and even a seersucker suit in light blue with a straw boater hat. The suit still had sales tags hanging from it.

"Well, I can't wear these new things till all the tags are cut off. "

He looked quickly at Mina's eyes, then her hand, and then at me. He paused, turned, walked away, turned back to us and began talking again. He announced to us that as living proof that the Incarnation was a viable process, he would be the spokesman for what he called "the media and public relations campaign" that he envisioned for the new company he was going to build around the Incarnación. I listened, spellbound as this spastic looking young man described his formula for success. He handed us papers he had already had prepared for us, and gave each of us a special envelope bearing our names. "These contain your pay for the work you have done."

He made eye contact with me.

"They also contain an offer to stay with me and ride the rocket to the future of medicine!"

He handed out the last of the envelopes. I opened mine. I had become an instant multi-millionaire. The first thing I thought about when I realized that I had four and a half million dollars to spend as I pleased was that I could finally afford to have my old motorcycle professionally restored. The paint I put on it was never really right.

So there I was in lala land when I noticed that William Ichabod Nelson was shaking my hand, congratulating Minerva and I on our engagement. When I looked into his eyes, I was trying not to show my amusement at the preposterous image of this punk offering me his blessing to marry what looked like his older sister.

The young and extremely perceptive William Ichabod said, "I *am* still Mina's father, Victor."

"I know. Thank you." I said, immediately averting my gaze.

But I guess the damage was done. I felt embarrassed for not being aloof and professional or acclimating myself to the present state of the man. I missed the old Elvin, even though he was destined to die. But Minerva loved the new William just as much as she did the old Elvin. I could not blame her. He was energetic, intelligent, and funny. So I had to get used to the prospect of having a father - in -law younger than myself. I regretted that I did not know the original Elvin better, so that I could compare the new and old versions of this amusing person. In many ways, young people can be as stodgy and crotchety as their grandparents, and we all know how the elderly can be perfectly immature. This William Ichabod was both at the same time.

Young William Ichabod was still experiencing occasional muscular spasms and stiffness of the joints, which he attributed, in the most caustic tones, to the atrophied condition of Henry Davis Nelson, Elvin's sister's son.

"He was a vegetable! He was a weakling!"

Despite these distractions, William decided to proceed with his schedule, and was planning for us all to attend a formal dinner event the very next night. This was to take place in a banquet hall in a posh hotel and would feature a lecture by Elvin Williams, who would be announcing to the world a revolutionary surgical procedure developed by his specialized laboratory.

W. Ichabod had decided that since no announcement of the death of Elvin Williams had been made, people could be invited to see what was supposed to be his first public appearance since his heart surgery.

Minerva told me that Elvin would occasionally give lectures on his botanical discoveries, and were known in the industry as "Elvin's nickelodeon," because he always treated his audience to a slide show presentation of photos of his latest trip into the jungle. He was an amateur photographer of note, and had even published a coffee-table book of photos of the jungle. I felt as though I had gotten to know the man a little bit, and I eagerly anticipated the opportunity to see him on a stage.

I remember getting dressed, because Minerva and William Ichabod had bought me a suit to wear to the function. It fit really well and actually made me feel comfortable being dressed up, a sensation I was unaccustomed to.

That night we all ate a delicious dinner and wondered, a bit uneasily, what William Ichabod Nelson was doing behind the stage. Then the lights went down and the casual music ensemble gradually lowered its volume. For some reason, I was looking around at all the faces illuminated by the candles on the tables. I saw Pat and Wally and without smiling, I waved to them, and they waved back. So did Minerva.

I turned back toward the stage and William was there. He coughed near the microphone and listened to its echo in the giant room.

He seemed to be steadying himself by holding onto the podium as he looked into the pale glow of the banquet hall. He peered closely, now, into the shadows, and was able to recognize business and academic associates, and he smiled at all the people.

He nodded toward Pat and Wally, who seemed confused. I don't think they knew who Ichabod was at that point.

Then Ichabod's eyes settled on Minerva. He looked at her for so long that people at nearby tables noticed, and turned to look at us as well. The following is a transcript of his speech as it was rather accurately published later   – in a tabloid trash magazine and is copied here - without their permission (so sue me).

"Allow me to introduce myself. My name is William Ichabod Nelson. You may have not heard of me, and that is only natural, for I did not exist two months ago. You were invited here tonight to hear a lecture by Elvin Gettysburg Williams III, but I must regret to inform you that you are the victims of a prevarication, and furthermore, that the King, as he was known, is no longer with us. He has, if you will pardon the pun, left the building! Don't be alarmed! I knew Elvin better than anyone else here, and I know for a fact that he wants me here now, speaking on his behalf.

"Some people seem happy and content to survive for a while, and work for a while, and then die. These people are abundant, and that's a damned good thing for us all! But for some people, mere survival is not enough. Some of us have a dream, and a few of us will pursue our dream for an entire lifetime. This was the Elvin I knew, who pursued his dream for an entire exciting and rewarding lifetime, then died, and then proceeded, after death, to realize his dream. I know what you're thinking! You are all thinking, 'is this man mad? Did he just say that he realized his dream after he died?' Well, it's true. I, Elvin, discovered the secret of how to enjoy a new life even as my old and hollow body dehydrates in a freezer, even as I speak."

"After a lifetime of searching, I, as Elvin found people capable of doing the impossible, on schedule, and they, the people whose land we are exploiting, whose resources we rape, the Yohimbe, or the Earth People, had pity on us! And they sent this great boon, this Incarnación as a gift, an offering of truly universal love, as a way of saving their forest home, for themselves, for the animals, and plants, and indeed, all of us on this fragile planet that we seem to hate so much. I can personally attest to the efficacy of the treatment that Elvin discovered, for I was the first subject of what will undoubtedly become the most revolutionary surgical procedure since the Caesarian section. And now I will, with your permission, disrobe, so that you may fully appreciate the magnitude of the Incarnación in all its glory."

At this point William quickly removed his suit, removed the microphone from the podium, and turned his back to us. This caused an alarm quieted only by what he said next. He pointed up at the screen, and paced the stage in all his natural and unnatural glory as he expounded:

"Down my back you can see the scar that resulted from the transplanting of the brain and spinal cord of Elvin Williams into my young and fit new body. Please start the video, Chandrath. Thank you."

"Here is a series of scenes of the operation being performed in the jungle, as the Yohimbe do it. And don't get any bright ideas! I have worked out an exclusive agreement with them and they will not even reveal themselves to anyone but one of my agents. This historical operation was performed by Doctor Victor Germaine, who is seated there, next to his fiancée, my daughter, Minerva."

At this point he had turned and waved at us. There was a confused smattering of applause, and we both felt mortified. People near us seemed to glare in confusion.

"In this operation you see the brain and spine of a human being implanted into the body of a leopard... And here you see my operation, in a modern laboratory. There is Elvin on the left and that is the body you now see before you on the right. See here the removal of everything that made Elvin unique among men from the worn out body that was failing to serve him. And here this very same nervous system is being implanted in its new home. Here I am recovering. Smile for the camera! And now! Would 'ya just look at me!"

The slide show was over, and the screen turned a brilliant white, with William Ichabod framed in the light. William stretched out into an athletic pose, reaching for the stars and, as absurd as he looked, in that moment seemed to be the master of his own endless universe. His presentation was having an amazing effect on the crowd. Many people were disturbed by his stark nudity, but the jagged tattoo on William's back mesmerized them and they shut up. A man near me gagged and nearly vomited, and managed to get a glass of water to his lips while continuing to stare at me. For the most part, the audience was dumbfounded by William Ichabod Nelson. But some people began to whisper, then ask questions,

"Is this some kind of hoax?"

"What the hell is this?"

"Is Elvin dead?"

Then William was at the podium again. He put the microphone in its holder, and he had put his pants back on. He tugged a shirt across his back, and looked down at his hands as he buttoned it. As he manipulated the buttons, he spoke quietly, almost to himself.

"First of all, let me explain my name. I had always assumed that I would remain Elvin after the operation, but everything feels so different now, and a whole new range of possibilities stretches out before me, and it needs to be connected to a new name. So I have

decided that my new name shall be William Ichabod Nelson. It
functions at many levels. I want my name to be seen as a metaphor.
Williams was Elvin's old last name. Now it is my new first name.
Thus the cycle remains unbroken" This last part he said very quickly.

"And Ichabod. Ichabod. I've always liked the name Ichabod, and
I don't know why. It's just so pretty! So pretty. The Greek word for
fish was icthes, spelled: I-C-T-H-E-S. And fishes all come from water,
all of them, even the coelecanth. And did you not see for yourselves
how the Incarnación take place in water? You see that, don't you?
The fish was also the secret symbol for Jesus among the early
Christians. Christ was resurrected after death through the miracle of
God's divine will. And as it was apparently God's divine will that I be
able to resurrect myself, so I have taken as my own the symbolic
name of the resurrected. So behold the new man, son of himself!"

Someone near me said, "This is insane!"
Other people were on their cell phones, whispering quickly.
I looked at Minerva, who was spellbound by William. She sat
motionlessly staring, with her mouth actually open, as if she were
going to speak. I could not decide whether Minerva was terrified or
proud of her father. I certainly was not able to decide for myself. I
worried that he would collapse, or become totally incoherent, or do
something really bizarre. He continued speaking and his tone became
deeper, slower.

"And finally, there is the last name, Nelson. It was the last name
of my late sister's son, who ended his life in a coma induced by a
tragic drug overdose. I promised my sister that I would do everything
in my power to save her son, to see him walk again. Well I have, and
I think it's a shame that she is not here to see how wonderful her little
boy looks today. My sister told me that her son was irreplaceable.
And that reminds me of the medicine men who taught me the uses of
the herbs and potions that I have brought to modern civilization at
such reasonable prices over the years. The Yohimbe Secret Shamanic

Counsel was specific. This operation, this Incarnación was only intended to maintain the life of an irreplaceable man in the tribe. And in our modern, civilized society, are not all of us endowed with the possibility of being important to the group? Are we not all, each of us, Irreplaceable? You see, the Yohimbe women have always had their babies in secret villages, far from the main camp. No man is welcome, because the women believe that a man in the presence of a woman giving birth could project his spirit into the newborn and "take it over." And they probably could! So the Yohimbe men have kept the power of the Incarnación unto themselves. But my daughter Mina was able to convince the Jaguar-Yohimbe to reveal their secrets to us, and to the women of their own tribe. Thus, we have brought this gift to not only all of civilization, but to the female members of the Yohimbe people as well, a development perhaps as auspicious for the Yohimbe as the discovery is for us."

The man who called himself Ichabod had missed one button at the bottom of his shirt and ended up with an extra one at the top. He held it out and stared at it and was momentarily cross-eyed as he tried to focus on the offending button. Someone laughed out loud, nervously.

"Laughter is good!" William shouted, looking up, "Don't get me wrong! I am not asking for your praise, I am only here to claim your gratitude! I have risked *everything* for you, *my very life, in fact.*" He shouted this last bit, and the microphone blasted the words out and they echoed in the hall. Many people flinched and looked around. William stared out at the crowd, and there was a moment of absolute silence. I think that the audience was actually grasping the magnitude of William's presentation, or like Minerva and I, they were simply speechless. He pointed limply at an elderly gentleman in the front and asked him,

"Would you like to live your life over again, but as a young man?"
He swung around and waved at a very old woman.
"Hi there! Yes, you, how much would you pay to live again, all

over again, in a beautiful young body, knowing all that you know?"
But before there was an answer, William turned away, and said,
"Wait."
"*Wait!*" he repeated.
William gazed into the slide projector light. "Oh, shit! I have a
small confession to make."

At first his eyes squinted in the glare, but then he relaxed, and
seemed to gaze into the lamp. And we all waited to hear his next
words.
"Earlier this night, before any of you got to this room, I noticed a
piano backstage. I needed to sit down, and the bench looked just
right. So I walked over to it and I sat down. And I found the sensation
…charming… and I could feel the pedals under my feet, and I worked
them a few times, and I heard the mechanism go 'clunk, clunk.' So I
lifted the cover, and it slid back into the console. And there they
were… I watched in total amazement as my hands floated up to this
row of beautiful black and white keys, and began playing music. I
have no idea what it was, some sort of classical music, but it was
beautiful. I played for a while, listening to the music and actually
feeling the piano tremble! I was momentarily transported and held in
an endless rapture of musically induced euphoria. Then it stopped. I
could not remember the next part of this passage. So I sat there,
trying to remember, was it Chopin? And I played a bit of the music
again. And I tried to listen, to remember what the next note was,
which key to strike, when I realized, I don't remember the next friggin'
note because I never played the piano, I mean Elvin Gettysburg
Williams never played the damned piano! And I wondered just what
the hell was going on!"

I looked at Minerva, who turned to look at me. I looked back at
William. He had raised his hands in front of himself and was looking
at them, grinning at them.
"I looked at these hands, and it did not take me long to understand,
oh my brothers! I realized that my *nephew* played the piano! Yes he

did. And how do I know this? Well I'll tell you how I know this. I know that my nephew played the piano because *I paid for his God-damned piano lessons* ten years ago!"

At this point William began to struggle against an invisible force, and he seemed to push out with his hands as if he were in a box. I had seen him have terrible muscular contractions during his recovery, and had administered antispasmodics via injection. They made him drowsy. I had a pre-packaged dose with me and when I saw what was happening to William I stood and pulled the dose out of my pocket. I tore its paper package open. Minerva was rising as well. William noticed us and rotated his body to halt our progress.

"Wait. I'll be alright. This is merely an adverse side effect—and these spasms are getting more bearable all the time—in fact—everything is perfect! The operation will be duplicated, perfected, tested and fully sanctioned by all concerned regulatory agencies."

He tried to smile, and made a strange face.

"An excellent investment opportunity!"

Here his voice became quiet and he appeared to become weak. Minerva and I now approached the slowly wilting young man. Still in his socks, William looked pathetic. He tilted his head towards us as we approached. He spoke into the microphone as if he was a captured spy and the microphone was the only weapon he had left.

"Wait! Don't give me that, Victor."

I stopped and held my distance, and I saw that William was serious.

"I can't trust you anymore, Victor. Not since I have discovered that, since my reincorporation, certain officers of my company have, unbeknownst to me, moved to block the exercise of my executive privileges of my own company! Yes! A stealthy cabal of my own associates has decided that it would be best for the company if my 'Exact Identity' could be ascertained! So I ask you how exactly does a man identify himself to someone else? I cannot even be sure that I can identify myself to myself!

"You people don't understand what it's like to be me! I feel like I have been zipped into a sleeping bag with a stranger! I feel like I'm inhaling the smoke of someone else's cigarette! I watch as the business that I built, throughout a lifetime of tribulations and small victories, is being dismantled by lawyers. And to think that I gave these people express instructions, *express instructions* to transfer executive control only to a person to be named after the death of Elvin Williams, who would correctly answer questions to those who held a sealed envelope containing the correct answers! I guess that they knew they could trick me. Now they deny that such a plan ever existed. I hate to admit it, but they may all be right! Oh my God! What have I done? Don't follow me in here! This is like a potato that explodes in the oven and coats the hot metal with steaming starches and papery skin!

"Oh, thank you for coming to my party, but I'm so embarrassed! I had no idea it would end up like this! It's so hard to clean. And my eyes!"

At this moment he winced and appeared ready to faint. Minerva ran to his side, and with a terrifying speed William rotated and pushed Minerva back. She fell back onto her arm and nearly broke it. People shouted, and I lunged forward to assist Minerva. William had taken up the microphone and was rolling his head in an ugly way and leering at the standing, horror-stricken audience.

He growled, "Well I have some good news, and some bad news! The good news is that I have discovered and brought to civilization a surgical process that will change the course of human destiny and challenge the very need for a mother, or even a divine creator, who, by the way, reveals yet more and more of his face every day!

"The bad news is that I have ended up in the ultimate haunted house! I barely knew this kid! It's like being in a room with the radio on and the television on, while you're trying to read! I am having a hard time remembering what I am like! I'm scared. I want more heroin. My body remembers heroin."

Finally Chandrath appeared next to William, and William allowed himself to be led away by him, out to his limousine.

I stayed with Minerva, who was crying and shaking. There had been a lot of flash photography, but I had not noticed it until then. Suddenly it was extremely distracting. I remember that a lot of people crowded around Minerva and I, as we tried to follow William. People wanted to know all sorts of inane things, like what kind of drugs William was on, or if I was marrying Minerva for her money. One woman was asking over and over if I was a "Christless blasphemer," like Ichabod.

We finally managed to get into the limousine with William and Chandrath, and back to our lab. We did not speak for a long while and then we began asking each other a lot of questions, and Minerva was crying. "I was ready for him to live or die, but I never let myself imagine anything like *this.*"

I told her that I understood, that no one could have expected something this awful to happen.

Chandrath told me that I was wrong and his voice was shaking. "*You* tried to warn him Victor! Elvin laughed at you when you told him that he needed to exorcise Henry's body!"

We moved William from the laboratory into his house in Rancho Santa Fe. Elvin had lived there for thirty years, and I assumed that the familiar surroundings would appease William. The mansion was in the modern Southern California ranch style, spread out over an acre of partially attached rooms with gardens and trees between them. Orange trees and silver-gray Eucalyptus surrounded the house, which scented the air with their sweet and turpentine odors. There was also a staff of nurses and special attendants to assist William, and a security guard, hired just in time, by Chandrath.

Chapter 12: Los Perdidos

William's mental condition continued to deteriorate. He exhibited dis-associative schizoid episodes with alternating bouts of self and other-directed violent behavior. Sometimes he was clearly hallucinating, and at other times seemed to have muscular contractions and motor skill problems which may have been due to the recovery from the Incarnación. He often acted literally like an animal, crawling on his hands and knees, eating food only off a plate on the floor.

Later, when I went to visit him, the orderly warned me that William was behaving erratically. When I went into his suite I got my first look at the modifications that had been made to accommodate "The William," as I once heard someone call him. All the furniture was gone and soft pale orange-pink carpet extended up the walls to the ceiling. Other places were padded and covered with canvas. Thick plastic plates covered the windows. I think it was the same plastic material that the operating tank was made of. I wandered around the rooms, calling out William's name. Chandrath appeared under an arch that led to an adjoining hall. This was a huge room, possibly the biggest in the complex. The entire hall was one giant padded cell.

Chandrath quietly told me, "William is busy searching for Eight Jaguar on the astral plane. Trying to get an exorcism, I guess."

William was on the other end of the hall, squirming on the floor and singing in Spanish:

"Soy el Perdido, Ooy Hoy Hoy Hoyyy!"
"Yo Soy el Escondido, Ay Hay Hay Hayyyy!"

In San Diego, the radio receives Mexican stations, and we listened to them occasionally. They were very alien sounding to me. The Mexicans sing 'Hoyyy' and 'Hayyy' in their Mariachi songs, and here Elvin sounded strangely authentic, and for a moment the hall was filled with a sweet ringing echo of his strange nasal and then very gringo sounding voice.

He saw me. "Hey! You! You were there, tell me what the Jaguar likes. You remember! Tobacco doesn't work anymore!"

William jumped onto his knees and trotted over towards me, slapping his hands on the ground. Chandrath dropped into a sitting position on the floor and pulled on my shirt, and I sat next to him. William relaxed and looked at me.

"Look at this room! This used to have art, books, nice furniture! Where the hell is all that stuff! Rene Lalique candelabras! A bicycle advertisement lithograph from Paris, circa 1907. What did you do with them? Who chose this color for the carpet? It makes me want to puke!"

I was assuming that this was the Elvin half of Ichabod before me, because he was aware of the contents of the room as Elvin would have remembered. A good sign, I was thinking. Then Ichabod lowered his head and glared at me from under the ridge of his stained brow.

"Oh I remember y-you, you are the guy my uncle paid to have his brain put into my body. Body."

He grinned broadly now, and leaned aggressively at me, his head tilted slightly forward. I struggled to answer, not exactly sure if Ichabod really was, or was just pretending to be his nephew Henry. I decided to address his first request

"The Jaguar... likes butterflies. He tries to catch them in his paw."

It was a total guess, but I felt that I should humor the poor guy. William seemed to strain, to listen and consider, then he said, "Don't change the subject! You *are* the guy."

"Yes! I am the idiot that shoehorned one man's brain into another's body. I'm sorry... but you told me to do it, *Elvin!*"

William closed his eyes. "You are making this hard for me. You are trying to confuse me. Ohhhh. You are smart; you are winning."

Before I was ready for it, he hit me. Right in the solar plexus. I fell back flat on the floor and I was momentarily unable to breathe, then I gulped some air and tried to compose myself as quickly as I could. And in that moment immediately after he hit me, the three of us quickly looked at each other. Then Chandrath and I were staring at William. Chandrath told me to get away from William. Just as I moved, William swung his leg, trying to kick me. I lurched back and he fell forward, and Chandrath stuck him with a syringe. Chandrath must have studied karate or something, because he hit Ichabod with the sharp as fast as a scorpion sting. Icky looked at his thigh, and then began chanting,

"Get Mark! Get Mark!"

And his voice went hoarse, which was a reaction to the sedative, but it made him sound as if he had been chanting "Get Mark" for many hours, and needed a sip of water. We watched him wilt into slumber. Chandrath helped me up, and led me out of the room, back to the front door, and the orderly let us out. I was shaking.

Chandrath was crying. "We were friends."

I asked him how long he had been working with Elvin.

"Three years, preparing for this! I have believed in all of his magic and I planned my life around this whole thing, and now he is gone."

I tried to think of what to say. "You are a great doctor, Chandrath. You have played a critical part in this whole process, and you are probably our only hope for ever getting Elvin back."

"Bullshit! I am useless to him. He needs Mark. But I know Mark. He and Elvin never liked each other. Mark won't come back."

I waited a long time. "No, he probably won't, Chandrath. I don't think he knows..."

Chandrath walked away. "Then all hope is gone. Elvin is lost. I do not know who this Mr. William Ichabod thing is, and all I have is a broken heart."

Then he was gone. I found out later that he left his check behind as well.

Chapter 13: A Small Miracle

I guess everyone is familiar with the pictures of all of us that the tabloid press circulated. The various accounts of the speech at the presentation, and Mr. Nelson's nervous breakdown were actually surprisingly accurate, and we all ended up looking like a pack of sadistic ghouls. For the next few weeks, we were hounded by religious fundamentalists, who accused us of attempting to play God. They somehow figured out where Elvin lived, and somehow hacked into the company database, contacted all of our stockholders and warned them about making profits from "Satan's work." So the value of the company crashed, and the financial trouble began. The religious operatives flooded our email accounts with religious junk mail, including endless anti-abortion material. Some of them even camped outside the residence in Rancho Santa Fe, with giant posters and banners with scriptural quotes painted on them. One of the protesters actually looked like the bible-school image of Jesus, long light brown hair, white robe, sandals. At first, I wanted to have them chased away, but Minerva stopped me, looked out a window at them, and told me to leave them alone. She was smiling at them! They were gone after a few days, but they left their "John 3:15" signs and fast-food litter behind. I went out to the street to clean up the clutter after they were gone. I looked up and down the road. The neighboring properties were peaceful again : with avocados, oranges, or both growing on them, and horses in the fields.

The real excitement began when the police detectives showed up. Two of them, in black suits. They had apparently read the tabloids and conferred with county records, because they were aware of the facts that Elvin Williams had died; a death certificate had been issued based on the cessation of his heartbeat, and yet shortly afterwards, someone claiming to be him had appeared on the scene, in the form of a young man who had somehow miraculously recovered from a drug-induced coma and changed his name. There was also a name change document placed with the county a few days before, which needed clearing up. Minerva stopped them as they read from their notes.

"You are right. We are experiencing an entirely new situation, and only had the existing certificates and forms to work with. We tried to make the existing death certificate fit our situation. We want to help you understand what happened, because while it may look confusing now, in the future there will be a certificate that will enable 'the man' to keep track of the people who have been Incarnated."

Minerva led the detectives from the kitchen, down the long hall to the window into Elvin's padded suite, and as chance would have it, we could all see Elvin in there, behaving insane, as if on cue. We invited the officers into the lab, showed them the equipment we used in the operation, and played a videotape that Elvin had made about a month before the operation. In it, he outlined his theory for the operation, and stated his intention to have the Incarnación performed upon himself. He looked straight into the camera and said, "Hey, I want to live forever. Don't you?"

He went on to identify himself as Elvin (of sound mind), and he told the camera that he would soon be transferring his assets over to a young man who was currently in a coma. He held up the name change form. In a surreal moment, the camera slowly panned over to the bed that Henry was sleeping in, and back to Elvin. I had never seen the video before, or since. We also showed them portions of a videotape of the operation being performed. For some reason, watching the video nearly nauseated me. Minerva noticed my discomfort and used her eyebrows to silently signal me to get a grip on myself. Finally, the bewildered men took copies of the videos with them, and warned us that they may need to return for more information. Mina watched them leave, and seemed content that they would never come back.

During the next few weeks, I mourned the wreck of the experiment, the crushing of my chance to achieve the acclaim I had dreamed of ever since I was a teen. But my sorrow was tempered by reflection upon the fate of the experiment's unhappy subject. Ichabod's madness became a shroud that kept anyone from seeing him. Was he Henry? Was he still Elvin? But it did not matter. The creature was incapable of speech nearly all of the time. He groaned, grunted and sighed. He was usually highly sedated. He wore a diaper under his pajamas. Minerva could not visit him, and it probably would not have mattered to Ichabod, anyway. But I visited him. One day I was in the room with Ichabod. He was lying on the floor, looking out the window. I was reading a book from Elvin's boxed-up library aloud to the monster I had created. It was a book about jazz musicians. Sometimes he was very quiet and we were able to keep a strange, uneasy company.

Suddenly, I was startled by a loud noise. It was Ichabod, trying to talk. He was making short yelps, and pounding on the window, looking at something outside. At first I considered calling for assistance, but Ichabod was only interested in whatever he was seeing outside, and I did not feel as if I were in any danger, being near him. I think he was having trouble seeing out of one eye, because he was holding his hand over one eye, and straining to see with the other. So I went to where he was and I looked outside. There was nothing there. I looked down at Icky, and he was pawing at the window, and hissing with excitement. I looked again. There! Near some bushes, someone was standing on the side of the road, looking up at the house.

It almost seemed as if he were looking right at us. At first I thought it was a leftover religious zealot, but then it looked more like a homeless person—stringy hair, dirty clothes. I became concerned. In the little time I had spent there, I had learned one thing: there are no homeless people in Rancho Santa Fe. Or swimming-pool-less or multi-car-garage-less people, for that matter. Even the migrant avocado pickers had excellent barracks, with freshly made beds to sleep in, hot showers, good meals, and even cable TV. I decided to go out and see who the loiterer was. As I got to the far end of the room, I turned and looked back at Ichabod. He was looking at me, waving me out of the room, and he suddenly began speaking very quickly and clearly, telling me to get the person outside, and bring him in. I was so surprised to hear his voice again!

"Go! G-get hhhim!!!" W. I. hissed through his teeth.

I was not stupid; I took the security guard with me. I was telling him that I saw a suspicious person on the street, and just as I got to the end of the driveway, I heard Minerva's voice. She had already gotten there, and was leading the wretched looking man up the road, towards the house. She shouted out to us. "Look who it is! It's Mark!!!"

Sure enough. It was Mark, the anthropologist. I was so surprised to see him that I could barely speak. Mark put out his hand to shake as if we were meeting for the first time. "Hi I am Mark, the anthropologist!"

I liked that little touch. I put my feet together, stooped slightly at the waist, smiled and shook his hand. We both began laughing, and I hugged him.

"You stink!" I told him.

"I know!" he replied, "Some Mexicans let me ride in the back of the truck, with some pigs. Before that I had been walking for weeks!"

The ratty sneakers that he had on were completely blown out. Soon we were in the house. We led Mark to the private mental ward in the north wing of the house. The creature crawled over to the door, and what was once Elvin began to paw all over Mark's leg. "My, how you have changed!" Mark cooed to the Ichabeast. Mark lowered himself to the floor and looked seriously into the eyes of the Incarnated one.

"He is still in there," Mark announced.

Minerva burst out crying, which caught me off guard. I tried to comfort her, pulling her near with my arm around her shoulder. "He is not happy in there at all."

Mark turned to the creature. "Elvin! I will try to help you, but this is still Henry's body!"

The moment Mark said this, Ichabod made a fantastic pouncing leap at Mark, knocking him back. Mark executed a perfect judo flip, and the recycled man was sent crashing over onto his head. Ichabod landed hard, and we all rushed to help him up. He was unsure of what to do.

"Excellent motor skills!" Was all Mark said. He left the room.

Minerva told the nurse to use the sedative on her cousin-father. I followed Mark through the house and watched him. He was still so funny. He was acting like a tourist in a fancy hotel, peeking into closets, checking an antique for dust as if he was wearing a white glove. I remained silent, but he developed some small talk. "So is there a kitchen anywhere around here?"

I directed him back the way we had come. "Actually the house is easy to navigate…here's the kitchen."

Like a fiend, Mark opened the refrigerator and began to ravish a pan of lasagna with his dirty bare hands. I asked him if he wanted it heated in the microwave. "It would not take long."

He shook his head and requested beer by pointing at it and grunting with his mouth full of food. I got two, twisted off the caps, and grunted back at him. Minerva entered the room and watched Mark eat. She wrinkled her nose with exaggerated disgust. "You smell like dung…and onions."

Mark paused in his chewing, swallowed his bite of lasagna and added, "And urine! Yes, Mini, I know. I have got to get myself into a shower."

We all sat in silence, looking back and forth at each other. Then Mark got up, took his beer, and began to prowl around the place, looking out the windows. "There *is* one! I knew it."

In a flash, he was trotting outside, stripping off his shirt, which was a neat trick, because he still had the beer in his hand, which he had to switch back and forth. I was following him, and Mina was following me. Mark gave a hoot, and jumped into the swimming pool. By the time we got there, he was tossing his drenched pants up onto the pristine patio, and splashing about like a kid. He got some pool water In his beer.

"I'll go and get you some of Victor's clothes."

I called after her, "Fuck that! Get him one of Ichabod's cool new outfits!"

Minerva left as Mark was asking if Ichabod minded. I assured him that it was no inconvenience at all, and I pointed out that young William would not mind at all. At this point, Mark and I endured a short silence.

"So Mark! Did you really hitch-hike all the way here?"

He looked at me out of the sides of his eyes, making a really funny, secret-spy style face. I laughed a little bit, and I added, "And what in God's name ever possessed you to come back?"

Mark dropped the silly face, looked past me, and I could feel Mina behind me. She had brought some clothes, some soap, some shampoo, and a washcloth. Mark shampooed his hair as he told us the story. Mina and I sat on the edge and dangled our feet in the pool.

"Well, Victor, when I decided to stay with the jungle people, I figured that I would never ever return to the good ol' US of A. You gave me the GPS-beacon thing, and I almost got rid of it. I threw it into some bushes as we were leaving the Site of the Jaguar Dance. But when a Yohimbe kid noticed that I was not wearing it, she took some other kids back and hunted for it. They found it, and the girl wore it like a necklace! She had to show it to me and claim it for herself, according to Yohimbe custom, in front of everyone. I just ignored her. Life with them was fun. They treated me like family, and I helped them choose a new shaman, who turned out to be Sapac, of all people."

Minerva seemed astonished at this news. "But she…"

"That's right!" Mark turned to me, "Sapac is a female."

I was impressed.

"Well she was the Chief's daughter," Mina suggested.

"Yes, and very influential among the men folk," Mark added, wiggling his eyebrows.

At this point, Mark and Mina went into a detailed discussion relating to the pecking order among the women and the ranking of the ex-wives of the Chief. Many Yohimbe terms were used, and I wasn't able to follow the conversation, but Mina occasionally shouted out "Oh!" or "I can't believe it!" as if she were discussing gossip or a soap opera episode.

I interrupted, "So what caused you to leave, Mark?"

Mark paused. "Well, believe it or not …it was Elvin."

Mina and I eyed each other suspiciously.

"What exactly do you mean by 'it was Elvin'?" she asked.

"What I mean, Minerva, is that your crazy father invaded me on the frikking astral plane! He bombarded my dreams and begged me to come and help him get rid of Henry!"

"Bombarded your dreams?" I asked, rhetorically.

Mark looked from Minerva to me and back, then he told us how Elvin nearly drove him insane. "Well, it all started in a series of dreams that I had when we relocated the camp to a higher 'wet season' camp. The ladies of the tribe began to give me a lot of trance water, and I slept a lot. I dreamed about basic jungle technology, how to eat, where to hunt. Different members of the tribe were actually entering my dreams to show me things.

"It was very beautiful, and they fully accepted me, and treated me like a guest and a member at the same time, 'like a newborn baby,' they said. I loved those dreams, and I was happier that I have ever been. But then I became aware of something watching, from the bushes. At first I thought it was Chief Eight Jaguar. I deduced that the beast had died, and the man you sewed up inside it was then free to roam about in dreamland. But then my theory was shot when the animal in question showed up alive. It had been a week since we had moved into the new camp, and the hunters returned one evening with news of the footprints of a giant cat. The next day they followed them to a place where the sun showed through a clearing in the woods, over a fallen tree. This was just the sort of place the Chief liked to be. The tribe found other subtle signs of the Chief's Incarnated life. It was very difficult for them, even though they could not actually find the cat-person. Some of the tribe became terrified of the dark, and the group gathered very close together, and they clung to each other."

Minerva reminded me that normally the Yohimbe are not afraid of the dark.

Mark nodded in agreement. "Right, and they were all scared of the Jaguar Man. They acted like he was no longer their Chief, and some of the wives claimed that their ex-husband still wanted them as his wives.

"It takes a lot to unsettle a Yohimbe woman. So I was not at all sure what this thing in my dreams was, and I became almost afraid to go to sleep. I demanded that they stop making me take the trance water, and they did, and I was awake more often, but sometimes, even in conventional sleep, I would still be chased by some creepy force that always seemed just out of sight, in my peripheral vision, or behind me, behind a tree, around a corner. I told the tribe about it, and they seemed very concerned, not because they thought it was their Chief, but something else altogether. They told me that it would be extremely unlike their Chief to lurk about and not present himself. 'He would pounce on you!' one of the hunters told me, 'and rip your throat out,' said another. Then they told me that if I was haunted, I had to find out who or what it was that was haunting me. Then they gave me trance water one last time, and pretty much told me to clear it up with the dream-spirit, or they would kick me out."

"Out?" Mina asked him.

"Yes! Out, as in kicked out of the tribe! Out of the jungle! I was distraught as I fell asleep that last time. I had never had to act as an agent of will in my own dreams. To me, having a dream was like watching a movie, I rarely participated, and when I did it was pretty normal stuff. As soon as I was dreaming well, I realized that I was in a classroom. I was in the city college where I first studied anthropology, right after I got out of prison. It was a wonderful campus, and I still miss the place. Cute girls. This part of the dream was pleasant, but then I realized that I was not alone. I suddenly became very agitated, and I turned around fast as I could, just in time to see something move behind a wall. I crouched into a good Yohimbe stick-fighting stance, sort of a karate defensive pose, and I challenged whoever was behind the wall to come out and face me. And it was horrible! A shaggy stringy beast popped out. All I could see was his eyes. It looked like it was a giant mop that had been used to clean filth. It was slimy and stringy. It breathed and moved like a human. I was frozen with fear and disgust. I wanted to run, but you know how it is in a dream, I was stuck! The thing came close to me and began to pull the muck off of itself, but the crud kept returning. Again, and again, the strange monster kept pulling stuff off of itself, but the slimy crud kept returning. It was horrible to see."

"Then suddenly, I could see the face, and it was Elvin! He was trying to speak, but his mouth was full of the filth that covered him. He hissed at me and then staggered away, and I woke up. I was surrounded by Yohimbe, who told me that they had restrained me, because they could tell that I was trying to escape whatever I was confronting in my dream! I told them about Elvin, and they needed clarification. When they apprehended the fact that I was dreaming about the man, my - our boss, who had been Incarnated up here in the USA, they began to worry. An ex-wife of the Chief asked me if I was referring to Minerva's father. I confirmed this. Then they asked me if I thought that Elvin had exorcised the body of his host prior to his own operation. They already knew the answer when I said that I doubted whether Elvin could do it or would even care. They looked sad, and held my hands and told me that I had to leave. Immediately. I began to cry, and I asked them where I had to go, and they were suddenly very upset with me. 'You have to remove the host-spirit from your friend's body before it is too late!' is what Sapac said. I told her that I did not want to leave the jungle, and that Elvin was not really my friend, not my responsibility, and she looked at me with really deep shame. I was responsible, she told me, and they were afraid that I would lose my way if I did not go and help 'my friend' as she called Elvin. 'If you dream him here he will take you for his own, and you will haunt all of us! ' Sapac told me that just because the Yohimbe do not wear a watch, or sunglasses, they are civilized enough to know to be afraid of ghosts, just like me. 'You know how it is, they make people act crazy,' she told me. I tried to explain that I could deal with it here, in the jungle. 'No you can't!' She shouted up at me. I looked out across the faces of the tribe. Everyone was looking back at me as if I was infested with bubonic fleas. So I had to leave. I walked out of the jungle, escorted by hunters. Then I was alone."

"Where?" I asked.

"Somewhere in Southern Mexico. Chiapas."

Mini was looking at the growing ring of dirt in the pool around Mark.

"How did you survive?"

"Well, I got pretty hungry, but if you see some workers working, ask them if you can help. If you work hard, they will feed you." Mark told us that he spent seven days hitchhiking all the way to the border, and after a day-long delay at the border, had walked to the lab in Rancho Santa Fe. I was not adequately impressed, but Minerva refocused her glare at Mark and said, "That's like thirty miles, Mark!"

He in the pool, he with the shampoo lather crown, agreed, raising his eyebrows. "I walked a long way, Mini, but I did not have a heavy load. Just the clothes I was wearing.

"The people in Mexico treated me well. I always managed to get a ride. When I got to the border I felt an unexpected gladness to be back in the US, but when I got to customs I ran into some trouble because I had no identification on me!

"I was diverted into an interrogation area, and I tried to explain who I was. I attempted to call someone in the lab to claim me, and nobody, I mean NOBODY would talk to me. Whoever answered the phone had absolutely no idea who I was, or pretended not to know me."

Minerva and I looked at each other.

"Mark, the company has passed into a legal conservatorship pending the stockholders determination of either where Elvin is, or who that guy in the rubber room is. For now, they are denying any connection to the project."

Mark asked us how that was possible. "Everyone knows about it! The guys at the immigration office certainly know all about it, so when I claimed to be associated with the operation they actually debated whether the experiment was a hoax or not! One of them had a tabloid magazine featuring the story and photos of the presentation Elvin gave, and that seemed to make the argument more intense.

"They finally decided that my mother could come and identify me with my high school yearbook, of all things. They had to run all sorts of extra searches in their database, and she actually had to sign an affidavit of sponsorship, stating that I was indeed her son. She drove away afterward. Most humiliating!"

I asked Mark when he had been in prison. He did not seem to mind my asking. "Well, I was busted growing a large crop of high grade weed, and I did sixteen months. It was in prison that I began studying anthropology."

I asked him if he had discovered any wild people that were like prisoners. He told me that he thinks that the Yanomamo are very tough and brutal, so are the Mud Men of Borneo, but he has never seen anything like the Los Angeles gang -bangers. I laughed at his joke, but he seemed to be quite serious.

"The funny part is that Minerva wanted me to go to Mexico, and I did not really want to join her because Elvin and I never got along very well. She tricked me by telling me that the Yohimbe are real ass kickers!"

Minerva had been silent, but she was getting fidgety. I asked Mark exactly how he knew Elvin, and Minerva blurted out, "Victor, Mark was my boyfriend!"

That made me flinch with shock, and it made Mark laugh. "Mini, didn't you tell him? Mini has a way of getting people to do what she wants them to do; but don't worry, I am glad that she introduced me to the Yano, and… and I think you two make a great couple."

I said, "Thank you." So did Minerva.

Chapter 14: Saving Ichabod

Unfortunately, I cannot tell you much about the actual exorcism of our Ichabod Williams. It happened very quickly. Mark rested and tried to avoid Elvin. In some parts of the house we could hear him screaming in his padded area, trying to call Mark. He sounded pathetic, and we sat silently, listening and wondering how long he could wail. That night, Mark realized that he would be unable to sleep without Elvin invading his mind. I was in the kitchen with him. The light was dim and we were quiet. The mood in the room felt as if he were an astronaut, preparing to go to Pluto. He took some aspirin and ate even more food, and told me that he wished he could get more rest. He really did look tired. Minerva entered the kitchen and asked Mark if he knew what to do.

"I haven't got a clue," he whispered.

I asked Mark if he had ever witnessed an exorcism, and Minerva told me that no one ever saw the Chief perform an exorcism.

"But they did seem to believe that I could fix him," Mark said, "or at least they knew that I was responsible, or that I am the closest thing Elvin has to a savior."

When he left the room, Mina looked at me and asked, "a savior?"

Mark asked that I go in with him.

We stood by the door, and realized that it was silent inside the padded area. We listened as carefully as we could, and it was the first time that I ever saw Minerva act cautiously. She really was afraid of what was going on. We tiptoed around the padded rooms, hunting in a small pack. Long shadows crept across the floor near every window, and each shadow stenciled grey leaves and branches there.

"Maybe Ichabod fell asleep," I offered.

Mina listened more closely. She could hear him breathing. She signaled to Mark, who turned the corner and approached Ichabod. He spoke Ichabod's name aloud, then Elvin's, then Henry's, and got no response. He took two giant steps up to the sleeping person, crouched slowly, and put his hand on the Incarnated one's wrinkled, sweaty brow. We waited. Mark held his hand on Ichabod's forehead for a moment, then he signaled us to come closer. Minerva and I approached with caution and sat next to the cousin-dad. Mina and I began to pet his hair. We stopped. The boy woke up and smiled at us, but we could see that he was near tears with pain or madness. He was experiencing a manner of spastic convulsion that I have never seen anywhere else. He was physically shaking at a frequency that could not be discerned in the obscure light, but the moment I touched him, I could feel that his whole body was vibrating, ringing really, like a silent buzzer. He was shaking as if a mild electric current was burning through him.

Minerva began to get really upset as she felt the victim's condition. She was trying to brace his head, to hold his skull tightly, but it was useless. Ichabod lifted his head to look up at us, and his teeth were clenched down on a bloody sock.

Mark began telling Elvin to relax, to let go, to calm down. Elvin slowly nodded his head but the veins and muscles on his neck and head were tense and drawn to the breaking point.

"William Ichabod Nelson! Elvin Gettysburg Williams III! Both of you! Listen to me! This body can belong to neither of you now. Both of you must leave. You have been torturing each other long enough, guys! You are both good people, but you both made some really bad mistakes, and now you should just let each other go. Just let go."

And the tattooed man did just that. He breathed out a few sobs of grief and then began to relax. We took turns petting his head, and we watched as he slipped away. He stopped shaking, then he became like water. He fell asleep and then he kept falling.

"Check his pulse, Victor," Mark said.

"He's dead, I think." I felt his pulse at the carotid artery. The thump of life had been smooth after the operation, smooth and strong. When he was having the spasms, his heartbeat was difficult to feel, but seemed highly erratic. Then it got smooth and regular, but weakening. His pulse grew weaker and weaker, until I simply could not feel it any longer.

"What time is it?" Mark asked.

"4:14," said Mina.

Mark went to a desk in the lab and produced a death certificate. I have always wondered how he just happened to know where one would be. Then a coroner's hearse suddenly appeared in the driveway. Mina had called them on her cell phone while I filled out the paperwork. The fellows from the morgue took the body of William Ichabod and a copy of the death certificate. It all happened so fast.

Soon enough, the government investigation of our company intensified. Certain county, State and Federal agencies wanted further clarification of the events leading to the death of one Mr. Williams, and of the death of Henry Nelson as well. What was Mark's involvement? What happened to Elvin? What is Minerva's Social Security Number? There really were not enough answers to satisfy the county coroner, and the bodies of Elvin and his nephew became public property. They left the refrigerated brain and spine of Henry in the cold storage unit at the lab. The court ordered all of the members of the lab not to leave the area so that they could be available for "further questioning."

Corporate lawyers began to fight for control of the Incarnation process, and no one could cash their checks while ownership and identification issues are being settled. The corporation hired private detectives who snooped around the property, looked through the trash and behaved really strangely. The Food and Drug Administration claimed "stewardship" of William and Henry and claimed jurisdiction over the autopsies. Then we found out that the corpse of William had disappeared.

The government sent an agent to the lab and asked us if we had taken it for burial. Minerva became furious with the MIB when she learned that her father's body was missing. "How could you guys lose a corpse?"

He was silent.

"Locate the cadaver!" she yelled.

He dropped his pen, picked it up, and left, looking irritated.

Epilogue

The text of the manuscript that I began a several months ago in the hotel ends there. I did not know what else to add to it. Minerva says that being busy has indeed helped me not "be an ass" any more, so the initial reason for writing all of this has proven itself worthwhile. But now that it is all over, I have one more event to add to the story.

After William's death my life sped up quite a bit, and it is difficult to remember everything that happened, so I will cover only the main points here. Apparently Mina had prepared new identities for herself and me, and she convinced me that we should leave the lab, early one morning. She told Mark to go back to Mexico, and he did, willingly. He took a GPS/beacon reader, and should be able to follow it back to the kid who kept his emitter/necklace, and find his way back to the Yohimbe tribe.

When it was actually time for us to leave the lab complex, Mina pressed the button on the answering machine and left a new greeting, for the cops, presumably: "Hey we told you everything we know and you people keep bugging us and losing things. If you are too stupid to understand what happened, or if you simply can't believe it, then you can just go fuck yourselves!"

Her voice was so sweet.

After traveling from hotel to hotel for a few weeks, changing cars often and using a different series of credit cards to pay for things, we pulled up to a fantastic cabin in the woods. Up till that point, Mina had spent a lot of time looking in the rear-view mirror of the car, looking out the blinds of hotel windows, always looking for anyone who might be following us. Once we go to the cabin, however, Minerva relaxed. The place was left to Minerva byLillian and Art Cook, and Mina was finally sure that we were no longer being followed.

Mina is now very pregnant, and recently I almost blew our cover by revealing my knowledge of medicine to the local doctor, who was telling us "what to expect" during the delivery in the most patronizing of tones. I started asking him pointed questions about who would be placing the epidural, if there was a fetal heart monitor available, and I wanted to make sure that the blood work was handled by a decent lab. "She is, after all, O negative."

Mina scolded me for letting too much of myself slip out. "You are not a doctor any more, Victor!"

"I still know more than that quack."

"Your medical license was revoked last march."

"I still know more than that quack."

"If your ego gets us discovered by the government or the corporation, then I will have to leave you. You are a writer now."

And I have one last thing to write.

So I was sitting on my favorite log by the lake one day, looking at some ducks swimming along. There was a rustling of leaves beside me, and William Ichabod Nelson walked out of the brush, and sat on the log next to me. I was terrified and shocked. I could not speak. Or move. Ichabod had smeared makeup over the scars on his forehead. I was staring at the pasty-looking and poorly-matched cosmetic with bulging eyes, and I could barely hear him speak. Then I listened to him.

His voice was clear as a bell. "When Mark did his 'relaxation exorcism' thing on me, he merely put me into a trance that mimicked death, or he did a poor job of trying to kill me. Either way, it worked! All we had to do was get you to pronounce me dead. I woke up later, in a drawer at the morgue. It was latched from the outside, but who cares? The shakes were gone! I felt great. I began to sing to myself. "Then someone must have heard me and came and opened the drawer. The light washed over me, and I pushed the drawer open and sat up. Just then I saw someone, who was standing near, me fall right over. It was the security. He had passed out cold. Apparently he was drunk, and I suspect that he had a really hard time explaining his plight to his superiors after my escape. Maybe they had a videotape of my shenanigans to clear it all up. I found some clothes on a fresh corpse, and took them off him and put them on myself. It was like another Incarnación! As per our little emergency plan, Mark had put a necklace on me, and it held a safety deposit box key, with some supplies in it."

The wind began to murmur in the leaves.

"So who am I talking to, Ichabod?"

"Oh, its me, Elvin! The kid and I, we worked out some stuff. We are like Siamese twins now, and we get along just fine. He actually likes my brain, and I believe we have done wonders with Henry's old body. He still wants weed, and hey maybe we'll try it. At least we know there is no lethal dose."

"I'm glad that you two have something worked out."

Upon hearing those words, Ichabod's mood changed quickly, and he looked over his shoulder, then spoke to me in a conspiratorial way, telling me that he was going to return to Mexico, to be "maintained" by the Yohimbe doctors. He claimed that he is not really enjoying his second life, and cannot get his nephew's presence out of his head. He looked from left to right, and cocked his head to the side and listened to the creaking branches of the trees. He told me that while he was in the death trance that Mark had put him into, he saw everything "the way it really is" and he recommended that I read the Tibetan Book of the Dead.

I wondered if he remembered making fun of that book earlier. He congratulated me on the imminent birth of my daughter. He told me that I would make a fantastic dad because I have no ideas about what to do or how to act, saying, " You will be natural."

He thanked me for all the help. He said that someday he would return to say hello to Minerva, and that she should not worry about him.

"Tell her that I love her very much." He was crying.

Then he disappeared into the trees. I had not moved the whole time he was there.

As soon as I returned to our cabin, Minerva realized that I had seen something. She looked at me with a raised eyebrow. I could not hide it from her. I told her that I had seen Ichabod.

"Really?"

"Yeah, isn't it amazing?"

"Well, I was sort of expecting that. What did he say?"

"That he loves you."

She looked out the window for a while.

"Is your book finished yet?"

"Yes, except for this last little event."

"Then it is time for you to finish it. We are broke!"

Well, at least we have a home. The cabin is fantastic. I can't tell you where it is, but I can say that there is a small town down the road apiece, and in that small town is a small restaurant with a big faded red stop sign painted on the side of it that reads: "*STOP EAT DIRT CHEAP.*" They also sell bait. I love the town. Heck, I love all the small towns. I had never seen many small towns here in the US, until Mina took me on the "Journey of Cleansing," which is what she called our run from the law.

So now I live near a small town, and with a computer and satellite TV, and I don't think we miss a thing. Yes, life is very nice here and I look forward to winter. The locals are sure that it will snow.

Because the fiddlehead ferns came up early this year.

Printed in the United States
1455000001B/237